The Greatest ...

The
Fallen

The Fallen

The Greatest Sin #1

Lee French and Erik Kort

TANGLED
SKY
PRESS

Published by Tangled Sky Press
www.tangledskypress.com

First printing, January 2014

ISBN: 978-0-9891210-9-5

The Fallen is a work of fiction. Names, places, and incidents are either products of the authors' imaginations or used fictitiously.

Acknowledgments

Lee French

I wish to thank (in no particular order) squirrels, zombies, broccoli, the cluebat, and cheesecake for all their bountiful inspiration over the years. As for humans, Ian and Matt both influenced Chavali in ways that I am deeply grateful for. Gwen is the loveliest sounding board I could ever want.

Dana, Kerri, and Kim have my undying gratitude for their willingness to put up with my inane ramblings about self-doubt, tea, self-doubt, spam, and self-doubt. Troy has been a reliable source of the odd joy-filled moment stolen from the jaws of tedium. And, of course, my parents, John and Sally, have always been worthy of thanks, for most everything, even when I'm unwilling to admit it.

Erik Kort

Special thanks to Alex, who never thought I was wasting my life or time by spending hours upon hours on projects that would never earn me any money.

And to Mom and Dad, who always want to read what I've written even if it makes them cringe inside. Some day I'll write a children's book. With pictures. It'll be grand.

Other Books by the Authors

The Greatest Sin Series

The Fallen

Harbinger

Moon Shades (coming Spring 2015)

Lee French

Maze Beset Trilogy

Dragons In Pieces

Dragons In Chains

Dragons In Flight

In the Ilauris setting

Damsel In Distress

Shadow & Spice (short story)

Spirit Knights

Girls Can't Be Knights (coming June 2015)

Erik Kort

(as Erik Marshall)

Wards of the Thicket

Children Without Faces

Children Without Voices (coming Winter 2015)

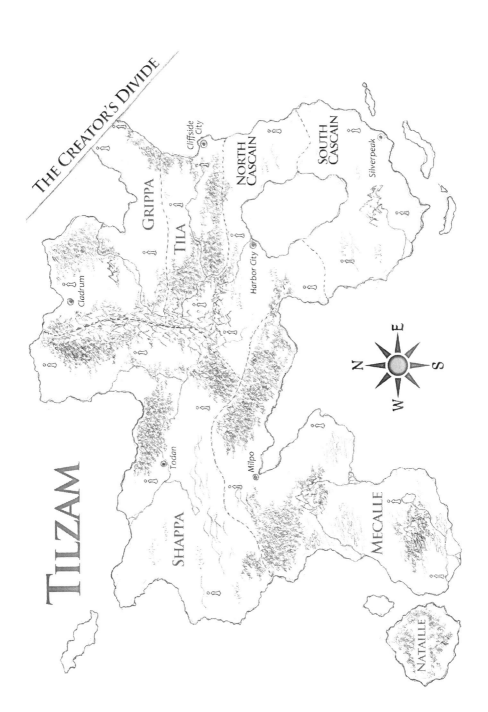

THE CREATOR'S DIVIDE

TILZAM

GRIPPA

TILA

Cladrum

SHAPPA

Todan

Milpo

Harbor City

Cliffside City

NORTH CASCAIN

SOUTH CASCAIN

Silverpeak

MECAILLE

NATAILLE

N
E
S
W

Prologue

Long ago when the world was young, the Creator looked out over the landscape. It was quiet, peaceful, and tranquil. This pleased the Creator. Time passed and the silence began to gnaw at the Creator—no longer did it bring pleasure. So the Creator's hand stretched out and touched the world, and all manner of growing things—flowers and vines, grasses and trees—sprang forth. The sounds of their growth brought pleasure once more to the Creator.

Soon, the steady sound of growing was no longer enough, so the Creator touched the world once more. Birds and animals sprang forth from the plants and the world was filled with the din of their life. This pleased the Creator immensely, so much that the Creator touched the world once more. Woman and man together emerged from the same fruit and their laughter was the sweetest thing yet.

In this way, all intelligent and living things were created to fill the silence that had plagued the Creator for so long. And for a time and another time, it was enough and the Creator wandered the world, taking pleasure in its life.

All good things come to an end.

One day, the Creator looked out again and the sight brought no pleasure, only disgust. The budding people of the world were sinning and it was the most wretched thing in the eyes of the Creator. "Begone from me!" the Creator cried. The peoples of the world were driven before the angry Creator. Out of their homes they fled, away from the sight of their god. Mountains rose up behind them and a great voice cried out in anguish. "You have done something terrible in the sight of your God! As punishment, you will be driven from the land of your fathers to the wilderness beyond. You will not see my face again until you learn to atone for your sins and repent!"

Great towers sprang from the earth all across the land, great crystals at their tips glowing in the night. "Behold, these shall stand as testimony to you and your children. They will watch you and keep you from doing what is evil. Keep watch and teach those after you to follow in the ways of peace. Repent or you will perish alone and forsaken by your god!" Then, behind them, a great wall of shining light burst from the ground. Those who dared to touch it were wreathed in flame and darkness and, from that day forth, no one saw the Creator again.

—A memory shared by every sentient being across Tilzam from birth

Chapter 1

"I swear on Estevior's soul that this color matches your feather," Pasha said solemnly, brandishing a brush laden with nail polish. She nodded to the long, thin feather grafted into her sister's skull just above her left eyebrow, tattoos around it making it look as if an exotic flower sprouted from her forehead.

Chavali snorted. "And if it doesn't, it's your fault for making me look stupid." When Pasha moved to pick up her hand, Chavali threw a small piece of thin silk at her. "I don't want to hear your thoughts right now. I can tell what's in them easily enough."

The younger woman stuck out her tongue, but picked up the cloth and used it to keep their skin from touching. She set to the task of painting Chavali's fingernails. "You don't know, you're just saying that."

Smirking, Chavali leaned her chin on her free hand as her elbow rested on her table. It brought her closer, so she could speak softer and more intimately. "You want Amets to bend you over a stump and—"

"Okay, okay," Pasha interrupted with an exasperated huff, "maybe you do. Show-off."

"Tomorrow is the Feast, you should find him then. After you dance, you'll be all flushed and sweaty already anyway. Might as well throw yourself at him." Keeping the sourness out of that statement presented a challenge. Chavali made the effort for Pasha. She would never bother for anyone else.

"Mmm." Pasha applied herself to her task without another word.

Chavali arched an eyebrow and considered pressing further. It would, however, accomplish nothing. Instead, she threaded the fingers of her free hand through the spirits, coaxing them into producing an illusion for her. It was the only thing she could actually control about the spirits, and she reveled in that control. If she wanted to make it actually look good tomorrow night, though, she needed someone else's opinion. "Is this good for flesh tone?" The image in the air showed a random man of the clan. He had an amalgamation of their basic shared features: dark hair, dark eyes, light olive skin, strong chin, sharp nose. She also used the typical clansman body type, with broad shoulders and noticeable muscle.

Pasha glanced at the image, took a second look, and smirked as she returned to painting the polish on Chavali's nails. "No, it's a little too green. Is that supposed to be Keino?"

"No." Chavali adjusted the color and let her mouth twist into something between a smirk and a scowl. "Estevior."

"That's better. He looks like Keino, though."

"All the men look the same," she grumbled, then modified the image so it resembled Papá more.

"I'm sure there's nothing to read in the fact that your version of the First Blaukenev looks like your bodyguard," Pasha said with and innocent smile. She set her brush aside and blew gently on Chavali's fingernails to get them to dry faster. "I'm done. Try not to chip it before the Feast."

"Shut up." Chavali's face fell into a full scowl. She stood when Pasha did, swishing her hands through the air to dry her nails and dismiss the illusion. Pasha looked at her and giggled. The sound of her girlish tittering pushed Chavali's annoyance away. She chose to be grateful for it, as their carnival would open soon anyway; her job demanded her look mysterious and strange, not unapproachable.

Pasha pushed the tent flap open, and Chavali had to blink several times to adjust to the bright sunlight outside. Today was a glorious day. Surely, something wretched would happen to ruin it before long. Nothing could ever be a pure pleasure.

With the thought, she saw the thing holding the greatest chance of turning this day into a disaster. Keino stood outside her tent, a silent sentinel set for her safety. Rather, he remained silent while performing that duty in front of Outsiders. The rest of the time, she only wished he'd shut up. Watching Pasha run off in the sunshine made her want to do something rude to Keino for the sake of mischief. Knowing the impulse to be irrational and silly, she restrained herself for now.

"Fetch Amets for me," Chavali ordered. "I need to speak with him."

Keino flicked his eyes from Pasha's back to Chavali's chest. Her costume bared more of her neck and chest than her usual garb without making her feel indecent. His gaze always went there first when she wore it. His eyes flicked up to her face when he opened his mouth. "You should do it yourself. The walk will put you in a better mood."

She sneered at him. "Or the walk might annoy me, because it'll mean I don't have time to do anything else."

"What do you need him for, anyway?" To most people, it would sound like nothing more that a casually curious question. Chavali knew better. his mouth tightened at the corners and his inflections of the words carried a tiny hint of sulking.

"None of your business." She gestured in imperious dismissal. "Just go get him."

For a moment, she thought Keino would start an argument for the sake of starting an argument. Then he turned and stalked away. Behind his back, Chavali rolled her eyes and paced across the camp in a different direction. It was arranged in circles, with a firepit in the center, tents in a small ring around that, an empty ring around that for people to walk in, then more tents in an outer ring and the wagons surrounding that. They set the camp up this way anytime the clan chose to camp near a place to do business. In the wilderness or near a village to small to have coin worth taking, they didn't bother with the tents.

Her own tent, placed in the center ring where it couldn't be seen from the wide gap set to face the town, had enough space for her table and two stools. Today, they camped in Tila, having crossed the border yesterday from Grippa. They would dawdle in Tila until the clan elders decided to leave, then probably go around the mountains to Shappa. Chavali didn't care. No matter how the people of each country claimed to be all very different, everyone had the same worries and hopes and dreams and fears.

Mamá had a large wooden cup of sun-brewed tea ready for her when she got back to the family wagon. It was made with orange peels and cloves and something else she didn't know the name of, and would keep her thirst in check until she stopped for lunch. "They just left to go tell the townies we're here," Laisa told her, pushing the cup into her hands while carefully avoiding actual physical contact. "No time for dawdling."

That was for the best, as Chavali didn't particularly want to hear anything her mother had to say this morning. Clutching her cup, her steps took her quickly back to her tent, where she found Keino just returning with Amets in tow. She didn't see what was so special about him—he was rather average looking for the clan—as to get Pasha in a twist, but she wasn't going to question the younger woman's taste.

"Amets," she said pleasantly, turning a little to intercept him and separate him from Keino.

He smiled politely. She knew it was a smile only given because it was expected. Dealing with her didn't normally elicit pleasure from her kin. However, she commanded respect from the rest of the clan for her station and the burden she bore. "What do you need from me this morning?" He asked like he would gladly lay down his life right now if she commanded it, but she knew that wasn't true.

Carefully avoiding touching the part of his arm with bare skin, she prodded a little to take him into her confidence. "If you have any interest at all in bedding Pasha, you should ask her tomorrow at the Feast."

Amets blinked and stared at her, opened his mouth and shut it. Then he broke into a goofy grin. "Oh. Really?"

"No," Chavali rolled her eyes and snorted, "I'm asking you to rape my sister. Yes, of course. Have you never noticed her watching you?" It was a stupid question. Obviously, he never noticed or he would have asked her by now. Men. They had the observation skills of walnuts.

Her manner made him chuckle, but tentatively, like he wasn't sure it was a proper response and feared offending her. "No, I didn't."

Giving him a little shove to get him back to work, she called after him, "Wait until after she dances, I don't want her to miss that."

"Yeah," he called over his shoulder, "alright. Have a good day, then."

For the moment, she was Pasha's big sister, a non-scary person who just wanted Pasha to have a good time. This would evaporate long before she chanced to wind up in his presence again, just like it did with everyone else. That was no great mystery, she understood what they all saw when they looked at her. Once, it hurt, in a way, but she was over that by now.

She turned...and there was Keino, doing his best impression of a possessive lover. For four years so far, since the clan decided to do carnivals again, he had the duty of watching over her and handling anyone who got rowdy at the Seer. In that time, he managed to convince himself he was in love with her, the bastard.

"What was that about?"

Breezing past him, she pushed her tent open and went inside. "Still none of your business." She sat delicately on the lacquered stump that was her stool, leaned onto her small round table and set her cup by her feet. The top of the table was painted with various nonsense runes, some of it done by her, most by her predecessors. From her childhood, she knew there were a few she couldn't see anymore—the colors were the same shade as the table and she couldn't see color anymore, not since she got the feather. Likewise, she couldn't see most of the pattern she knew was in the rug acting as the tent's floor.

Much to her annoyance, he followed her inside. "He's not right for you, Chavali, he won't even let you touch him."

Though she enjoyed watching him squirm, especially in this particular way, there wasn't really time to savor it right now. "Don't be a moron," she snapped.

"What's that supposed to mean?" He crossed his arms, a picture of petulant irritation.

This was not the best way to get into a proper mood to handle mucking about in the minds of strangers. "Keino." She said his name with a heavy dose of exasperation and fingered the pendant of her necklace to avoid smacking him. "We've had this conversation before, I don't want to have it again right now. People will be here soon."

Keino scuffed a boot on the rug in frustration and let his hands fall to his side. "Why does everything always have to be complicated with you? I like you, you like me, that's all that should matter."

If only things were that simple. She watched him with a frown as he slipped onto the other seat and leaned on the table, mirroring her. It put their faces close together, close enough to kiss her with just a little effort. How much she actually wanted that was distracting. She put her effort into resisting his pull instead of answering him.

Gently, tenderly, he reached out and touched her hair. She let him get to the point of running two fingers along the feather lashed to a lock of hair before leaning away from him with a sigh. Looking away uncomfortably, she crossed her arms. "I don't want you to touch me. I don't want to know what you're thinking. It's bad enough I spend all day wading through the stupid thoughts of all these idiots who traipse through my tent without having to put up with whatever you want, too."

He sighed and pulled his hand back, let it fall limply to the table. "That's not fair."

"Fair?" She almost slapped him for that, but words could handle that just as well as her hand. Better, even, because he might misinterpret her hand. "At what point did you decide life was fair? 'Fair' is for children and morons," she sneered. "No, Keino, it's not fair at all."

His hand darted out and seized hers. *Is this really so bad, really so horrible? I want you Chavali, I've wanted you for so long, to be mine.* With it, she was also privy to the highly explicit images in his head, of all the things he wanted to do to her, most without any interest at all in whether she wanted it done to her or not. *I've watched you grow and blossom into the woman you are, and-*

"Get out," she snarled and yanked her hand away to get out of that ramble. "Go whine about your tragic heartbreak to someone else. I am not yours, I never will be, and no amount of persistence on your part will change that."

He sat there, glaring at her while she glared right back at him, for a good ten seconds or so, then got up like he wanted to kick something and stormed out. Chavali drew in a deep breath and let it out very slowly, closing her eyes and covering her face with both hands. Some day, he would give up. Until then, confrontations like this would keep happening. What a wonderful thing to look forward to for the rest of her life. Because she felt certain that growing older would do nothing to change any of this. He was already twenty-six, a year older than her. His fixation wasn't going to go away because of something as trifling as time.

Two more deep breaths solidified her control enough that she wasn't going to snap at the paying customers for no reason. Putting her hands down on her table, she was as ready as she'd ever be, and didn't have long to wait before the first sucker poked his head in. The fee for her services was high enough to keep out the merely curious, but low enough that most could afford it if they really wanted to. The clan promised a glimpse into the future, solutions to problems, and answers to questions. She delivered them. In a sense.

"Come in." They did not speak the clan tongue in front of Outsiders, not without dire need, lest someone overhear enough to translate it and learn it. Instead, they spoke Shappan, the dominant language of Tilzam. Nearly everyone knew it, regardless of country or native tongue. Along with the words, spoken in the light accent of the clan, she lifted a hand to gesture to the stool opposite herself. "You are welcome here."

He was timid as a mouse and small like one, too. Keino could probably lift this man over his head with one hand, or break him in half over his knee. Chavali watched him take small steps and dart his eyes all around. "Um, you're the Seer?" His Shappan was obviously better than her own, she could tell even with so few words spoken.

"Yes. No one can see into the tent, it is safe, you are safe here. Sit, be calm." Coaxing a scared little man onto the seat was not her preferred way to spend her time, and she stifled a sigh and a roll of her eyes. "If you do not sit, I cannot help, yes?"

"Oh, right. Of course." He moved quickly, practically jumped onto the stool while shooting terrified looks all around the tent. "I've just never done anything like this before, and, um, I'm worried about..."

Holding out her hand, she kept her tone calm and patient. "Give me your hand. I cannot help if I have no connection to you."

His audible gulp made her want to roll her eyes again, but he tentatively offered her his hand. As she seized it, the spirits rushed him, eager as always for new people to interact with. *DearCreatorIhopeyoucanhelpmeI'mdoomedthisissocrazy*

"Calm," she told him, shutting her eyes to make it easier to focus on this pile of crap. "If you do not calm down, I see nothing, just a bouncing jumble of nervous. Deep breath in through your nose, out through your mouth. Come, do this a few times."

His thoughts began to settle as he followed her orders. It became less a rushed mush and more actual coherent ideas. *Amy is going to kill me for this. I shouldn't be doubting her, but I am, and I need to fix that. She's a sweet girl, this is all my fault.*

"I see a name. A-something, Anna? No, Amy. Does this name mean something to you?"

As expected, he gasped a little. *How does she know that? Is this the real thing? If she knows that, she must know if she's seeing Marcus or not.* "Yes, that's my wife."

"You worry about her, you think she is meeting someone else?"

"Yes!" His mind flooded with images of Amy, who he loved, deeply, but also with images of a man much more virile than himself. That other man wore armor and used a blade for his work. A city guard, perhaps, or a soldier.

"There is another name, with a...'c'. But not at the front, maybe in the end? No, no, the middle. Arcu, Marcus. Yes, Marcus. He wields authority."

"Yes, he's in the Order of the Strong Arm, one of their knights. I need to know." He already knew, of course. That was the beauty of what Chavali did. All the answers were in his mind already, he just needed someone else to say it out loud because he couldn't, the poor fool. People really were the same no matter where she went.

Still, it wasn't good to just say things like this aloud with no feeling or props, or anything to give her an air of more authority than just pulling things out of the air. Her free hand dipped into the pouch tied to the thin belt around her waist, pulled out five objects at random, and tossed them on the table. Keeping hold of his hand, she peered down at the bones, finding it amusing that all five were actually bones. The pouch also had crystals, stones, and even bits of shell and wood, all minimally shaped and etched with ink-stained runes by her own hand.

It wasn't that the bones were only props—they had meaning for Chavali. It was that they weren't tools for divining. In this context, she used them as prompts, as ideas for how to word things. "Mmm." Starting with the one closest to him, because she didn't like having them out of her control for any longer than necessary, she picked up a chicken wing bone, displayed it, then deposited it back into her pouch. "Pain of the soul, for you." The next was a finger bone, from Seer Marika's dead body. "Betrayal. Face down, the betrayer is a woman." A bone from the paw of a dog was next. She liked that dog enough to preserve a part of him. "Love, but face down, so actually just lust."

This was all so stupid and predictable. His mind raced as her words confirmed everything he feared. The next, a horse's tooth, was an amusing addition. "Secrets. Many secrets." The last one almost always turned up when she did this. It was a chunk of unidentified bone, picked up some time ago just because of its odd shape. "Fear. There is much fear through all of this."

She needed nothing more from this man to make her pronouncement, and she didn't care in the slightest if it turned out to be true or not. They would be gone tomorrow morning, and likely wouldn't return for several years, if ever. Letting go of his hand, she gave him a mildly sympathetic look. "The bones have spoken. She has betrayed you, and you must deal with that in your own way. The bones, I think, suggest you confront it head-on, but this Marcus may not be wise to cross."

He nodded, resigned. "Thank you."

"It is not a thing I wish to be thanked for. Good fortune to you." She watched him get up and leave, and snorted at him as soon as the tent flap was shut again. Idiot. He was, of course, the first of today's parade of idiots and twits, each of them with a story as uninteresting as the next, a story Chavali had heard dozens of times before. It wasn't until late in the day that anything of real interest crossed her path.

The woman was an elf. This in itself was not unusual, nor was her apparent wealth. Chavali saw all kinds—the clan treasured coin far more than prejudice. Moving hesitantly, the elf sat down at the table with her bag clutched like she expected someone to appear and snatch it from her at any moment. Her hair was swept up in an elegant coif, her dress made of fine cloth and cut to suit her slim frame. She wore no jewelry, suggesting at least some wits between her pointed ears—this was no place to flaunt money like that.

"I am in need of discreet assistance." She didn't look at Chavali, kept her eyes on the table and her hands to herself.

Chavali nodded, used to this kind of concern. "I do not leave my clan nor gossip to one client about another, you are safe here." This woman was skeptical, but she came anyway. Perhaps the price was the reason—it didn't cost much to see a fortune teller, not compared to a diviner or priest. Holding out her hand, she said gently, "Your hand, please. I must make a connection to tell you anything of value."

The woman looked at Chavali's hand, her mouth puckered with distaste like she just swallowed a lemon. "I would rather hear what you have to say without one."

Raising an eyebrow, Chavali looked the woman over again, careful-ly this time. More of a skeptic than she thought. Time to do what she could with nothing more than body language and behavior to go on. "None of it will be terribly useful or specific to you. I do not peddle miracles or spin power, I merely read what there is to be seen in the aura and threads of fate. Without being able to touch your skin, my sight is limited to vagaries and generalizations. However, I can tell already that you are used to people doing what you tell them to, used to control. Right now, something is spinning out of your control, and you seek answers to make it bend to your will."

Her delicate blond brows furrowed. "You're guessing."

Chavali shrugged, unconcerned. "I did just say it will not be very helpful if you will not let me take your hand. Vague and general. I have no connection to you at all, not even your name, how do you expect me to throw the bones for you if I know nothing?" She watched the woman's canted eyes focus on her hand, still not wanting to take it. Anyone who said she didn't work for the clan had no idea what she did in here. "I swear to you on the souls of the clan that no word of what happens here will leave this tent through my lips. I will not judge you, nor will the rest of the clan." That second part was a bald-faced lie, but they wouldn't do it to her face, at least.

"Yliana," she said as she hesitantly slipped her hand into Chavali's.

The Seer opened her mouth to politely acknowledge the introduction—Yliana seemed the type to appreciate that kind of gesture—when it happened. Her vision clouded over with purple, making her curse in the clan's language. That was short and clipped, though, as she didn't have time to get creative with insulting anything before the spirits took over. She hated it when this happened, but it was part of being the Seer. They decided which words she would say, holding her rigid until they were done with her.

"Eyes of blue. Taken from you. Mountain view. Dreams askew. Burning through."

When it was done, Chavali sucked in a breath and slumped against the table, yanked her hand away from Yliana. It wouldn't happen again, but the woman got more than she paid for already. A second later, the purple film left her vision and the expected agony exploded in her head. "Keino, I need tea," she croaked out, her own voice loud enough to cause her more pain.

"What happened?" Yliana was breathless, and though her voice was barely above a whisper, it still hurt to hear.

"Ma'am," Keino's voice said from the tent flap, "come with me, please."

Thank everything for him at times like this. Yliana left her tent, and outside, Keino would give her a basic explanation of how to interpret what she just heard, then send her on her way. All Chavali had to do was suffer through this for five minutes or so. It felt like someone cracked open her skull with a pickaxe, then poured in a bucket of glass shards and jumped up and down on her head with boots made of spikes, while beating a very large drum right next to each of her ears. All of that didn't quite explain how intensely excruciating this torture was, but it was close.

Shutting her eyes didn't help, holding her head didn't help, breathing deeply didn't help. She did all of those things anyway. The alternative was doing nothing, which made the waiting even worse than it had to be. Five hundred years later, or so it felt, Biholtz rushed in to do her job. She pushed Chavali's head back and helped her drink the tea. The girl knew enough to try to keep her mind as blank as possible while doing so, and let go as soon as Chavali choked down the last of the repulsive brew.

Another eon passed in agony. The pain receded to slowly for her tastes. As soon as it became tolerable, Chavali found herself as she often did under these circumstances: lying face up on the rug, Biholtz sitting quietly next to her with the empty cup and watching to see if anything went wrong.

"I'm fine," Chavali said.

Despite her mere twelve years, Biholtz had a very good stern, skeptical look. "Are you sure?" She offered Chavali a biscuit slathered in apricot jam.

Sitting up slowly, Chavali took the treat and shoved it into her mouth. These little dollops of sweetness chased away much of the disgusting taste of that brew. A swallow of her regular tea would finish the job.

Without being asked, Biholtz found her cup of regular tea under the table and offered it to her. "It's not too early to give up for today."

Taking a small drink of the tea, Chavali shrugged. "Tell Keino I'm done, but if anyone is willing to wait an hour or so, I'll still see them then."

Biholtz nodded and left. Chavali stayed sitting on the rug. She rubbed her face, wishing—for nothing. Wishing was stupid, of course. The spirits did what they did, and she had no say over it. She wasn't really a person anymore. When she became the Seer, she also became a vehicle. Chavali The Wagon hauled them around and stopped whenever they told her to. They climbed out and did things while she waited for them to wreak havoc and jump back in so she could get underway again.

Wallowing in self-pity would accomplish nothing, so she stood up and made her way out of the tent, intent on taking a walk while the queer numbness caused by the painkilling tea wore off. It wasn't really a proper medicinal brew. It had mustard seed and rosemary, ginger and radish leaf, and more. All of it together tasted like raw sewage. For whatever reason, it placated the spirits. Seer Marika's blend had been different but similar, the basis they used when experimenting to find what worked for Chavali.

Right after a prophecy, she always wondered why she had to be the one they chose for this. Why her? Papá told her that Marika considered her the best choice. Even without the spirits, she knew that to be a lie. He knew something and refused to tell her, something that would explain everything.

The first time she suffered through a prophecy, it took an hour to recover without the proper tea blend. She went on a rampage, demanding that someone to explain to her the reason it had to be her to endure this suffering. Any girl in the clan could have shouldered this burden. Fifteen-year-old Chavali had screamed and raged until her voice went hoarse.

"Accept it," they told her. No matter how many times she asked, they said nothing else. Everyone had a role in the clan. This was hers. She hated that answer.

Chapter 2

She passed through the small crowd. It was a busy carnival today. From what she saw, the people here weren't desperate, but they didn't get many travelers of any kind here. Her clan was a rare treat, and they indulged in it. This was good for the clan and good for the coffers. Avoiding contact with the Outsiders, she reached the outer ring of wagons and walked around in the space near the horses, just breathing and moving her arms and legs.

Keino found her within a few minutes. "I took your sign down. You look tired."

He was trying to manage her, something she never liked. She paused and crossed her arms to stare at him. "I'm not." Actually, she was. Being ridden by the spirits to deliver a warning—or a prophecy, or whatever anyone wanted to call it—was tiring in itself. Add to that a long half day with stupidity and desperation and insecurity shoved at her, and she could use a nap. If it was anyone else, she would probably just agree and ask not to be bothered for an hour or so.

"Liar."

Chavali snorted. "Of course I'm a liar, it's my job."

Keino made a face, he thought that was a lousy answer. He also crossed his arms, mirroring her. "You shouldn't lie to me, not to clan."

"Don't lecture me." The warning came with a pointed finger. He didn't get to order her around, she had higher status in the clan than he did.

Letting out a huff, Keino threw his arms up in exasperation. "Do what you want. I just came to tell you that you're done until the feast tonight."

"And yet, you're still here."

He scowled and stalked away, swallowing whatever he wanted to say. She watched him—actually, his butt—until he was lost in the crowd. Pity she didn't get to see that part of him more. It was his best feature, mostly because she got to see it when he was leaving. Never mind that he had to arrive for that to happen. The idea of him walking up just to turn around without a word to grant her the view made her smirk as she went to her family's wagon.

Shucking the outer few layers of her costume, she set them aside and flopped down on the bed. Sleeping alone held very little allure for her, but everyone else had work to do right now. She shut her eyes and drifted off quickly, finding herself—as she often did—in a dream. Controlling her dreams was a skill she never found herself able to exercise, but she always felt present, as if someone personally showed her something she needed to pay attention to.

This time, she stood in a meadow with small purple flowers growing here and there. It was a bright, sunny day, the sky cloudless in the shade of gray that meant it had to be a deep blue. She remembered what it looked like as a child, before she became the new Seer, yet couldn't conjure it in her dreams. Even here, where her eyes had no part in the process, she still saw only shades of gray except for those tiny motes of purple, a color the spirits seemed to have an odd fondness for. Sometimes, she wondered if the afterlife was purple, or magic or the spirits themselves.

Walking from one nowhere to another, she noticed the sun setting. In the darkness, terrible things always prowled. More importantly, a small child walked ahead of her, and she needed to scoop it up and take it inside. Intent on this, she hurried, but found the child sped up as she did. Soon enough, they both ran, Chavali chasing after the toddler as fast as her legs could carry her. Somehow, it stayed just out of her reach, and it ignored her shouts.

Behind her, a formless shadow swept across the meadow, cold, calm, implacable, and unavoidable. Despite its inevitability, she ran anyway, still chasing the child that somehow managed to keep a step ahead. She leaped to catch the child, landing on it, wrapping her arms around it and hitting the ground in a roll to protect it. Her actions didn't matter, though. The darkness blew over them both, turning the child to ash. It crumbled in her arms.

The ash flew around her, swirling as she tried to get to her feet, making her cough and sputter, getting into her eyes and ears, and pushing her back down. "It's time to wake up," the ash told her in a whisper. "You need to get dressed for the Feast." That was Pasha's voice, specifically how she sounded when Chavali was privy to her thoughts. Of everyone, she knew her younger sister the best, and would recognize that mind voice anywhere, even in the throes of a nightmare.

Opening her eyes, she found Pasha sitting over her, holding her hand. "That dream couldn't have been too bad," the younger woman said cheerfully as she let Chavali's hand go and scooted away.

"No, not bad. Normal." Rubbing her face, Chavali sat up slowly. "It was the shadow one. You caught me before the part with the grinning man." She only had a few different dreams, and this one seemed to be about an end of the world scenario. There was some deranged man—all she knew of him was the grin. He wanted to destroy everything, and he controlled the shadow and used it to kill everyone and everything except her. It was the least upsetting of the dreams she had routinely.

"Oh, well, good." Pasha rummaged through the clothing chest and found Chavali's Feast costume. It was more revealing and less flamboyant than the one she wore for Outsiders, with three-quarter sleeves that hung off her shoulders and a tight bodice that displayed her cleavage to good effect. The skirts were layered and multicolored, reaching just past her knees. It was good for dancing, which she always ended up doing at some point.

Shrugging out of the dress she already wore, Chavali let Pasha dress her, amused by how much the younger woman enjoyed the task. "I wish I knew if it was a warning or not."

Pasha clucked her tongue. "If it is, it's a stupid warning. What kind of a warning doesn't tell you how to prepare, or how to avert a disaster? It's just gloom and doom. All you can do in response to that is dance and live and be happy until you can't anymore."

Chavali snorted in amusement. "Yes, well, perhaps as it gets closer, the dreams will be more helpful."

"That's fine, then. So long as it's vague, I'll just be merry and ignore it." Pasha tied off the vest, tucking the strings in between Chavali's breasts. There's no point in worrying about something you can't prevent.

It was fine for Pasha to feel that way, she wasn't the one having the stupid dreams. Ten years of this, and Chavali was starting to question her sanity. At first, they were nightmares, terrifying things she was forced to sit through every night. When this was all new, she awoke sweating, panting, even cursing or screaming. But time dulled it, and now she only had mild reactions to the worst of them, even when they were able to get all the way to completion.

Shrugging, Chavali moved her body to make sure Pasha didn't tie it too tight. "And waggle your bottom at Amets."

"Yep, and that." Pasha grinned and paced around her, straightening the skirts and tugging on the back. "It looks good to me. Keino will probably want to jump you."

Chavali scowled. "I don't care what he wants."

"Yeah, I noticed." Pasha tried to hide how amused she was by that, but failed horribly. "You know, maybe you just need to figure out how to make him stop thinking. I mean, if what he was actually thinking was all fuzzy happy about actually getting to have sex finally, maybe—"

"Stop." With a bonfire, the night wouldn't be cool enough to justify a shawl, so Chavali didn't pull one out. "I refuse to spend my effort on making him palatable."

"Okay, okay. I'm just saying that maybe you could use the sex as much as him."

Chavali rolled her eyes. "He has two hands. They're always there for him."

Pasha chuckled and sighed to tell her she was being difficult. "Seer Marika—"

"Was a different person." Chavali left the wagon, knowing Pasha would stop because she wouldn't want Keino to overhear it. "I'm not Seer Marika, and I don't wish to be."

Pasha threw her arms around her sister from behind and squeezed her. *I know, and I'm glad. Be merry, Chavali. Your stories fall flat when you're cranky. I could tickle you if it'll help.*

Patting the girl's arm, Chavali snorted. "I'm fine. Go, run off and find someplace to sit where Amets'll be able to stare at your chest."

Chapter 3

"The Feast of Estevior is a time of indulgence, it is a time of joy. For today, we celebrate the founding of our clan, we celebrate the First Blaukenev." Everyone knew this, of course—Chavali said the same thing every year to mark this celebration. Before she started doing it ten years ago, the previous clan Seer did it, and the one before her, and so on for a very long time, possibly all the way back to the founding itself. From many of the stories she knew, Estevior sounded like the kind of man who would have begun a holiday dedicated to himself. In other words, he was a true Blaukenev in every way.

"We all know how he faced the Divide and made his vows to forge the clan, those tales are told often. This one, though, speaks of other things, and I have not told it before." Chavali hid a smirk as the younger members of the clan leaned in, suddenly interested, while the older ones looked her over with skepticism. Normally, this time was used to reinforce the story of the Founding itself through one of the three tales about it.

"Estevior Blaukenev was once nothing more than a man. Heroes are not born ready to do their great deeds, and neither was Estevior." Careful listeners would note her quite intentional suggestion that he wasn't a hero. "Once upon a time, so long ago there are no books to tell of it, Estevior walked the land with nothing but a plain stick." She had one handy and gripped it as she stood in the flickering light of the bonfire. This was a tale best told on her feet.

Brandishing her stick, a piece of deadfall collected earlier in anticipation of this, she paced slowly back and forth in front of the crowd, matching her pace to the cadence of her speech. "It wasn't so different from this one." She didn't know a maple from a birch, had no idea what kind it was, just that it was unimpressive in its nearly four feet of length with clumps of lichen clinging to the bark. "He walked with all the purpose of a squirrel, flitting about the lands we know today as Tila and Grippa, searching for something without knowing what it was.

"Those lands were beset by a plague, one that threatened all the world if allowed to fester. This was before Estevior built his power enough to bless our clan, he had only a wisp of what he would one day command." Chavali twined her fingers through the strands of the spirits around her, pulling out of them an illusion of a man who looked rather like her father using his stick and little blasts of magical force to fight shambling figures.

"He struggled greatly to make his way, every challenge he faced forcing him to dig into the well of his power, forcing him to flex those muscles more and more." The image in front of her gained more and more of the shambling figures. The illusory man kept fighting them off. "One day, he met Istal." She added a woman to the fight, pacing in with a sword and rune stick, blasting the shambling figures and putting her back to the man's. This woman bore a fair resemblance to Chavali's mother, though Laisa would never be caught dead with a sword; she preferred a spear.

"She, too, was a wanderer, but had no doubt of her purpose as he did, for she was a defender of the weak and infirm, a champion of right-eousness and mercy. When that first battle was over, she slapped him across the face for stupidity. 'What kind of moron,' she asked, 'retreats into a place with nothing to put his back against?'. Surprised by her actions, but imme-diately attracted to her, he replied, 'The kind who has no other way to meet beautiful women than to be rescued by them.'" As Chavali spoke, she changed the images to complement her words, making them do what she said they were doing.

"Istal decided that, since he didn't dispute her assessment of him, she would give him a chance. This is fortunate for all of us, as had she not, the First Blaukenev may also have been the last. Estevior saw in her a wom-an after his own heart, one with power and strength enough to rival his own. A partner. He fought by her side, was moved by her devotion to her cause. Eventually, his lust was replaced by love, but it took effort to win her over, for she was skeptical.

"One dark day, before the plague was cleansed, they stood as the last defense of a keep, a place where ordinary people sought refuge from the infected." This part of the story felt a little disjointed when Seer Marika told it to her. When she tried to retell it herself, even just practicing in front of a mirror, she finally understood why: the spirits pressed on her. It was like they knew it was a lie but couldn't tell her what the truth of it was. Why they should care if it was true or not escaped her; it was just a story. Besides, the whole thing was probably a giant, grand lie anyway. She even held some doubt whether Estevior was a real person instead of being an amalgamation of several men, but saying so would earn her only grief. "It is said the plague was the first true manifestation of the Creator's displeasure, that it was a test for the people of Tilzam. If enough of us rose up against it and fought and bled for ourselves, we would pass the test.

"Estevior and Istal tried to rouse the able-bodied among those present to help defend themselves, tried to get others to take command of their fates, but to no avail. Together, yet alone, they stood against the onslaught on the roof of what is now a buried ruin." Her illusion showed the pair side-by-side on the battlements of a keep, then pulled out to show how it was a small building compared to the forces arrayed against it. "The situation was hopeless, but they refused to give up."

That battle was difficult to verbally do justice to. She let the illusion show the horror of their situation, show how they made fire rain down and the earth erupt from beneath and ice blow from one side and great winds gust from the other. "Though they were powerful and able to do much, Istal was crushed beneath a great stone flung at them. She wasn't killed, but seriously hurt.

"Estevior knelt beside her, ignoring the battle in favor of the woman he had grown to love, though he hadn't told her yet in words. 'Forget about me,' she growled at him, trapped under the stone. 'Save them'. 'No,' he shook his head defiantly. 'They can rot. Without you, I'm only half a man, hardly worth the clothes on my back. Without you, I don't care what happens to anyone else, not even myself.' He blasted the rock before she could protest more, it flew back into his own face, but he was determined and kept blasting until she was free.

"She was still hurt, but without the rock pinning her down they had enough magic between them to get her back on her feet. Unfortunately, by then, the advancing horde had been ignored long enough to be unstoppable without destroying the keep. 'These people are going to die no matter what we do,' Istal told him as she surveyed the battle again, no hope left in her. Estevior kissed her and then did the only thing he could: he asked the Creator for forgiveness and saved them both, but no one else.

"And thus is the tale of how Estevior was burdened with his demons so that he came to found our clan. It is the blood of innocents that forged our path, a sacrifice we must always strive to be worthy of." The clan applauded as she banished the illusion with a brush of her hand through it. There were two hundred and thirty-one of them, and their faces all looked impressed, at least a little, even the elders. Some days, she had the sense they weren't entirely pleased with her as the clan Seer, but today was not one of them.

Pasha bounced to her feet right away, and she rushed forward, grabbing her sister in a brazen embrace. The spirits drank greedily from the younger woman, siphoning off her thoughts and shoving them into Chavali's head against her will. She couldn't stop them, and gave up trying a long time ago. No one was ever hurt by it, unless she counted herself, who had to endure whatever anyone thought when they touched her.

It was great! I'm glad we do this after dinner or I'd be starving. As usual, Pasha's thoughts were coherent and enthusiastic. She pulled away quickly, running off to gather with the other dancers.

Chavali only smiled in response. Even Pasha, the most comfortable with her of the entire clan, was unnerved by her answering things only thought and not spoken aloud. Her smile slipped the moment Pasha's back was turned, because she knew who would be at her side any moment and wasn't looking forward to him crowding her all night. A quick glance around caught Keino talking to someone else, distracted from her.

She hurried away from the spot and got herself a cup of Auivel's special occasion tea. It had a complicated flavor and needed nothing added to it. Whatever was in it, a subject Chavali had no knowledge of or interest in, the drink was divine. A shame Aiuvel only made it three times a year, but one of them was Chavali's birthday, so she couldn't complain too much.

Steaming wooden cup in hand, she took a long look at the food still sitting out on tables, left over from the feast. People offered their appreciation of her story and its telling as she passed them, though no one touched her —it was all smiles and nods, a few words and nothing more. Picking up a few things, she popped a bit of pastry wrapped sausage into her mouth and looked around for where to sit and watch the dancers.

Papá saved her a seat, he caught her eye and patted the bench next to himself. As the Seer, she was afforded some comforts others had to get old to enjoy. Her feet took her that way, but only a few steps in that direction, she noticed Keino looking her way and taking a step towards her. He was the last person she wanted to put up with while watching Pasha dance, but it didn't matter where she went. He'd find her and sit, stand, lie down, or come up with some way to hover near her. No doubt, he felt urged on his quest to court her by that tale, a downside she considered beforehand but decided to ignore.

As soon as she settled on the bench between her father and one of the other clan leaders, smoothing out her colored skirts, Keino stepped in behind her and put his hands on her bare shoulders. She didn't like him doing that without warning, and he knew it. Her face fell into an irritated scowl. No one around her seemed to notice, a fact that only irritated her more.

That was a good story, I liked it. What will it take for you to see me like that, Chavali?

Chavali jerked an elbow back and hit him hard in the groin. She brightened a bit as he reacted predictably and let go. If Auivel's tea wasn't so good, she would toss the contents of her cup in his face for good measure. Instead, she used Papá's cup.

"Chala," Papá chided. He disapproved, yet a smirk ghosted at the corners of his mouth.

"He knows better," she snapped.

"You aren't even giving him a chance."

"He's already had plenty of chances." She was saved from this old argument as the drumming began. A row of men sat to one side of the fire with drums made from animal skins stretched tight over gourds and baskets and other things, each one producing a different tone of thumping. They were practiced and set a complex beat for the ten women to dance around the bonfire to. Bodies jumped and swayed, arms waved and snapped, skirts twirled and bounced.

Chavali's eyes were drawn more to the play of shadows and fire on the ground than the people themselves. Something about the shapes made by the darkness called to her, it always had. She remembered finding them fascinating even before she was made the Seer. Now, 'hypnotic' was a better word for it.

The spell it cast over her wasn't broken until Pasha ran up and grabbed her hands, yanking her onto her feet. *Come dance with me, get your stick out of the mud!* The younger woman's excitement and joy flooded into Chavali, she let herself be whisked away without issue. Once, dancer was her intended path too, and she knew enough to make her colored skirts twirl and enjoy herself. They jumped and spun together, ignoring everything but the beating on the skins. It was a night for that, a night for wild abandon, a night that fell about nine months before the largest cluster of birthdays among the clan.

Despite what she did to him earlier, Keino stood at the fringes of the dancing, watching her, a bulge in his pants. His interest was both attractive and revolting; she wanted to tackle and devour him at the same time she wanted to slap that look of arrogant possessiveness right off his face and knee him in the balls. Again. Repeatedly.

Forget him, Pasha urged, pulling her around the fire so he couldn't watch as well from where he stood. Their hands clasped together. Her sister's mind fell into the pleasure of the dance, setting a second rhythm to it and putting them in synchronicity. Where it could have been awkward for the contact, it was instead a shared joy. For Pasha, she could make her big sister happy for a short time. For Chavali, she could push everything aside and have some blessed release.

At the best of times, it was difficult to truly forget Keino, but she did for a little while. He stayed out of their way and enough other clansfolk got up to lose themselves in the pounding of the drums to make him difficult to see. Neither of them could keep this up forever, though, and when Chavali let go of Pasha to go catch her breath and wipe the sweat from her face, she walked straight into Keino, who nearly leaped into her path.

Without a word, he seized her long hair and kissed her forcefully. *You want to be mine, you know you do. I want you, enough to forget what you did before. I will have you, Chavali, I will.*

Were it not for his thoughts, shoved into her mind no matter how much she didn't want them, she would have kissed him back, would have relaxed and enjoyed him. But she couldn't control that any more than she could control the sun or the moon. Was it really asking so much to be able to shut that off for a short time, long enough to take what she wanted from him? Yes, it was. She didn't control the spirits, they controlled her.

Jerking away from him, she stomped on his foot and slapped him, hard enough to leave a hand print across his face. "How dare you," she growled, fully aware they'd attracted the attention of everyone nearby. Expecting an apology, even a fake one, was too much like expecting snow in the summer, so she didn't wait around for one. Turning away and moving quickly enough to avoid his hand if he chose to try to stop her, she heard her father's voice as she pushed past the rest of the clan, telling Keino to leave her be to cool her temper. Thanks to Papá, of course, this would not be the end of it, but that was probably already true anyway.

She broke into a run to the outer edge of the camp. There, she stopped and leaned against the solid wood of a wagon, staring out at the blank darkness and drawing in deep, calming breaths. If there was one thing she would never be, it was his. Arrogant, infuriating bastard. That he was the only man in the clan not even remotely disturbed by her made him bold, obnoxious. He knew he had no competition. He knew he could do whatever he wanted and eventually she would relent just for lack of other options.

Unless, of course, she decided she didn't need a man for anything. That option was the one she chose, the one she resigned herself to and cried over years ago. It was a choice no one in the clan really understood, except maybe Pasha. She even still thought there might be a way. It was the only choice she could make, though. Bad enough she had to be privy to everyone else's thoughts when they touched her, worse that she couldn't stop it, not even for sex. And imagine what it would be like to carry a child! Would she be immune because it was part of her, or would she know the moment it began to form thoughts and be bombarded with them, unable to prevent it from driving her mad for even a moment until it was born?

"Chavali?"

She rolled her eyes and grimaced at the sound of her mother's voice. "Yes, Mamá," she answered, hiding how little she wanted to be noticed. "I'm here."

Laisa looked much as Chavali did, and Pasha too, only older. Where the two sisters had brown hair, barely tinted with dark red and reaching a few inches past their shoulders, their mother's was streaked with gray. All three had the same dark brown eyes, though Laisa's looked more tired, with lines around them. Laisa's mouth, though, and Pasha's, turned up at the corners, made them both look as if they found joy in all things. Chavali's turned down —she always looked surly without trying.

"Talk to me, Chala."

The pet name made her scowl again—if they wanted to call her 'Chala', they should have just named her that. "I have nothing to say that I haven't said before." Crossing her arms, she glared at nothing in particular.

"Keino is very upset." Laisa had a brown shawl thrown over her shoulders, it was something she did when she expected or hoped to wind up hugging Chavali. The sight of it annoyed her daughter more. It was a kind of rejection, a kind she hated to get from her own mother.

"Yes, let's all be sympathetic to Keino," she spat. "He only wants to tame the Seer for the good of the clan. Our kind will go extinct if he can't get her to spread her legs for him."

"Chavali," Laisa chided. "He's a man. You can't expect him to be a saint."

This argument was hardly new, and Chavali narrowed her eyes, uninterested in having it again. "I can, however, expect him not to be an ass." She pushed herself off the wagon and stalked away to find more solitude.

"You're so angry, Chala, maybe it's because you're alone."

She stopped and looked over her shoulder. "Or maybe it's because I'm never allowed to be."

Laisa frowned, the expression didn't suit her. "Someday, that wish will be granted, and you'll regret it."

"I very much doubt that." Chavali paced away, headed for her family's wagon. No one would be inside it, and her mother didn't follow her. By the time any of them got back to it for the night, she should be asleep already. If she wasn't, she could easily pretend to be.

The inside of their wagon was much the same as the inside of any other family wagon —storage space and a single bed everyone piled onto. She could command her own wagon so no one's dreams invaded her own, but she would have to handle everything for it and would miss Pasha too much. Instead, she had a nightgown with a high neck and long sleeves, plus thin gloves and socks. On cold nights, it was fine. On warm nights, she envied everyone else for being able to wear as little as they pleased.

Pasha claimed the nightgown she changed into was a soft pink. Chavali didn't care. Before putting the gloves on, she carefully hung her gold necklace on the nail in the wall for that purpose. It belonged to every clan Seer before her, going back a very long time. Rune etchings covered the fat, round pendant so thoroughly, it had no space for her add even a tiny one of her own. She pulled the beads off the two locks of hair where they normally sat, untwined the other feather from its own lock, and held the one in her forehead out of the way so she could brush her hair. The second feather had been a gift from Pasha. She said it matched the other one. Each lacquered wood bead, on the other hand, had a meaning and a purpose.

Threading the beads and feather back into her hair and tying them off was an intricate enough task to settle her and clear her mind. Since she was the first one to bed, she tossed herself down in the middle. It was the softest part, and her parents usually claimed it. She and Pasha were always pushed to one side, Luken and his wife, Zuli, to the other. Not tonight.

Chapter 4

In the morning, Chavali woke before dawn. She tried to roll over and go back to sleep, but she and Pasha were all tangled up together, and trying to get back to sleep only woke her more. Pasha grumbled in her sleep, Laisa mumbled and flung out an arm to smack Pasha and shut her up. It hit Chavali in the face instead, letting her know her mother was dreaming about sex with someone other than her father.

Shoving the arm away, Chavali got up and quickly changed into a plain dress. They'd be traveling today, as soon as the clan was up and about, so she had no need for anything more elaborate. It only took her a few minutes and she was out the door, stretching and annoyed at how early it was. The sky to the east had the barest hint of orange light—it would be at least an hour before anyone else got up, probably two before the wagons were moving.

There wasn't much she could do to help prepare for the morning's departure with no one else around yet. Men would handle the benches and such things, that's what muscles were for. She did find a few cups left on the dew-soaked grass, a plate here and a shoe there. Gathering these things up, she tossed them into a box left out for the purpose. The contents would be sorted and dealt with later.

One of the children left a doll out, she bent over to pick it up and set it someplace to dry out. Some noise off to the side announced someone else was up and about, but she ignored it. If they wanted something from her, they'd say so. Mamá had clips she could use to hang the doll in plain sight so the child it belonged to would claim it, she went to get some without disturbing anyone. Halfway there, she noticed someone was moving towards her swiftly, and turned to see a man lowering his head to plow into her. It was too late for her to avoid him by then.

A broad shoulder slammed into her chest, knocked her down and smacked her head on the ground. Dazed by the assault, she wasn't able to resist while he grabbed her hair and hauled her up enough so he could crouch and hold a knife to her neck. "This is all your fault," he hissed in her ear, his mouth right beside it. "I lost everything because of you."

By the time her wits regrouped, he had her on her feet, one arm around her waist, the other still holding the small blade to her neck, yet managing to keep from having skin contact with her. In all her years of serving as clan Seer, this never happened to her before. People threatened her, yes. It happened. No one ever actually carried one of those threats out. Rather, if they tried, someone—Keino—stopped them before it got to this point.

Speaking of her bodyguard, she opened her mouth to shout for him. Her attacker quickly moved the blade, pressing the flat across her lips. "I wouldn't, Seer Chavali. My hand's liable to slip." He mocked and threatened her at the same time, which didn't bode well.

"What do you want?" Her fear of him and his knife was easily kept under control and hidden under a thick layer of disdain.

"You ruined my life."

"I highly doubt that," she sneered. "Only a fool—" While she could hide her fear from him, she couldn't deny that when he tightened his grip on her waist, her mouth went dry and the words died in her throat. There wasn't much she could do about this, wasn't anything she could think of to get away from him without getting herself cut, probably badly.

"A fool, that's what you think? I'm a fool." He barked out a mirthless laugh. "Maybe I am. That doesn't excuse what you did to me." He started pulling her backwards, toward the opening in the wagons. If he got her away from here, things would go very badly for her, she knew that.

Keeping him talking was the only thing she could think to do. If she kept him busy long enough, someone else would wake up and come out. Anyone would be a help to her. "And what was that?"

He made a chiding 'tsk' sound. "Here I thought you were a Seer."

It was a risk, but she grabbed his hand to try to pull the knife away. At the same time that she took advantage of his surprise, she caught his thoughts, full of righteous rage, all directed at her. This man seethed with deep, dark, venomous hatred for her. There was a woman involved, his lover, or perhaps his wife. He loved her, with all his heart. She was dead now, and he was broken because of it. He blamed Chavali for her death.

While that was interesting, Chavali felt it was more important that his hand was away from her neck. "Keino!" Her shriek was less his name and more just as loud a noise as she could muster. It really didn't matter who heard her, so long as they came out with a weapon in hand. She only called for him specifically because dealing with this kind of thing was his job, and she was as used to that as he was.

The shout cost her. She saw it in his mind even as he moved the knife back to her neck and pressed the point hard enough to draw a bit of blood. Shying away from the blade pressed her body closer to his, giving him a better grip around her waist and a better chance to slip away with her. To her very great relief, she heard a few doors bang open and saw movement. The man—she hadn't seen his face and didn't recognize his voice or find anything in his mind to tell her who he was—stopped moving as he heard the sounds, too. Fortunately, they were still several feet away from leaving the ring of wagons. Everyone coming out would see them, easily.

"Anyone comes closer and I cut her head off!" He meant this threat, it was serious. As much as Chavali wanted to help them defuse this situation, she couldn't. Opening her mouth would force that blade through her flesh.

"If you harm her," Keino's voice rumbled dangerously from behind him, "I will do things to you that will make you wish you were dead."

Hearing his voice made Chavali flush with relief despite how much panic surged in her assailant's mind. As annoying as he was, as much as she wished he would leave her alone, he was the one person she trusted to be able to handle something like this. It filled her heart that when she called for him, he came. He was still an ass, but one that would take care of her, no matter what.

The attacker whirled her around as he spun to face Keino. She tried to resist, but wasn't very effective—instead of making him stumble, she made him move around her. "Back off," he growled, though she noted he was scared. And why shouldn't he be? Keino was a well-muscled man, just now holding his favorite curved blade and wearing nothing but a pair of loose pants and a vicious scowl. Under other circumstances, Chavali would admire the view.

"You will not leave this camp, ever, if you do not release her. Let go now and walk away." From the look in his eyes, Chavali felt quite certain there was no possible way Keino was just going to stand aside while this man ran away with his tail between his legs. Probably, he'd use that fist, the one his free hand was clenched into so hard his knuckles went white, and beat the man until he stopped moving. He might even use the sword to kill him regardless, because it was, in some ways, easiest to deal with a corpse.

Her attacker thought about the threat, sizing Keino up. He liked his chance in a fair fight, and didn't realize that while his attention was focused on Keino, other clansfolk edged towards the scene. This wouldn't be anything like a fair fight, not even close. The fool was actually trying to decide whether to cut her or not as he threw her to the ground.

Keino wasn't looking at her, so there was no way to try to tell him anything. Her attacker was likewise focused on Keino. She yanked on his hand to get the blade a little farther from her and twisted in his grip, forcing him to pay attention to her. It was all the opening Keino needed to throw his fist at the attacker's shoulder, hitting him hard enough to make him nearly drop the blade. With her now free to struggle in earnest, she wrenched herself down. He let go of her rather than be dragged with her.

Face down in the grass and making an effort to crawl away, she didn't see what happened, but she heard it well enough. There were grunts of effort, then the sharp crunch of bone was followed by a whimper of pain. Keino growled wordlessly, other people rushed towards the fight. It was over quickly, she looked up at a light touch on her back. Keino had spatters of blood on his skin but no injuries to produce them. Her attacker was swarmed by clan, leaving him free to check on her.

"It's okay, he's dead." He crouched down and she let him gather her up into his arms. "Are you hurt?"

Chavali reached up and swiped at her neck. It stung without enough pain to be serious. "Not really." Her fingers came away with a small smudge of blood. How irritating that her hand shook when she looked at it. She wasn't that pathetic, she didn't need to fall apart just because some deranged moron threatened her with a knife.

Keino took her hand in his and kissed it gently. *If I could kill him again for this, I would.*

For once, she let him hold her for more than a second or two without arguing about it or resisting. "I'm fine," she protested. His thoughts weren't annoying right now, and she really wanted to be held. No matter how little she wanted to admit it, sometimes she did want to be right here, with him, like this.

I will always be here for you. "Chavali." He liked saying her name and wanted her to know that.

She melted just a little bit for him. How could she not? That kind of promise was absurd, but exactly what she wanted to hear right now. Her stalwart defender would cross any distance, bridge any gap, go anywhere, do anything, all to protect her. "Thank you for coming when I called."

His smile was pleased. His thoughts showed her he wanted to kiss her, and were trundling down the road to sex. "I swear on Estevior, on clan, on everything, that I will always come for you." *I deserve you. I defended you. You're my right, my prize, my victory.* "Chavali, I lo—"

She pushed his face to turn his head away because he was moving in to kiss her. "Don't you dare say that," she growled. Of course his thoughts went that way. They always did.

"Why not? It's true." Refusing to let her go, he snapped his head back and pulled her closer. *Stop fighting me. You're mine, why can't you see that and submit?*

Struggling to get away from him just made her mood go more sour. "I'm not some kind of fragile doll you need to put in your bed and guard." She flung the words at his face, full of anger and frustration, and followed them with a wordless growl.

Stop it, if you'd just calm down and let me show you what I want, you'll want it too. "Chavali, quit it."

"Let go!" She was close to screaming into his ear at this point. All she wanted now was to be somewhere else, anywhere else. His arms tightened around her more, and she squirmed and fought against him more.

"Keino, let her go," Papá said. He was both stern and coaxing at the same time.

That was what it took to get him to make his arms go limp. Chavali tumbled back onto the grass. "I am not 'yours'." Someone took her hand and helped her stand, his mind urging her to be calm. The moment she was on her feet, she yanked her hand away and let it fly at Keino, slapping him hard enough to turn his head.

He didn't look at her. "I didn't say you were."

Chavali flung a hand out to express how stupid that statement was and stalked away. If it wasn't so ridiculous, she'd slap him again. That would, however, require staying there and continuing to deal with him. For one shining moment, he didn't want anything from her and she got what she needed. Then he had to go and spoil it.

"What happened?" Pasha yawned, still in her nightgown and only a few steps away from their wagon.

"Some moron came and gave Keino a chance to prove what an incredibly manly savior he is. Deserve," she spat. "He doesn't—" Pasha didn't need to hear this, and it wasn't fair to snap at her. "I just want him to leave me alone."

"Okay." Pasha was still half-asleep, she probably would agree to nearly anything. "I guess we're leaving early. Everyone is up now."

"Good. I want to be as far from here as possible as soon as possible." Getting away from Keino wasn't so easy, but at least she wouldn't have to look at him while they were moving.

Pasha hugged her sister. "Yeah, he's such an ass," she said absently, then flounced up the steps into their wagon to change her clothes.

Chapter 5

The wagon bounced over the bumpy dirt road. Hardly anyone used it, that was obvious. Tall grasses grew into it from both sides and the trees reached down enough to scrape the tops of the wagons. It was a sort of music, in a way, as the branches hit each wagon down the line, some of them breaking halfway through, others stubbornly holding on the whole time. The small gardens on top of some of the wagons probably were being damaged, but the clan would survive the loss of a few herbs and vegetables.

Chavali and Pasha sat together on the back of their family's wagon, feet dangling off the edge, unconcerned with the prospect of falling. Both had been doing this sort of thing since they were much younger, and could handle all but the most unexpected jostling. Behind their wagon, Amets drove his family's, making it difficult to keep Pasha on their task: doll making. They used dried husks from corn, wooden beads, smoothed sticks, and similar things to make dolls that would be sold to Outsiders. Clan children got much nicer ones. The task did a great deal to settle Chavali after this morning's events.

It was late afternoon, an hour or two before the clan would stop to make camp, when odd hoof beats coming from the rear of the caravan made both women look up and peer around the sides to catch a glimpse of what was going on. Chavali saw them and gestured to Pasha. "Horses with riders," she informed her sister, who crowded close, practically climbing on top of her.

The one in the front is cute. Too pale, though.

Chavali snorted. "Get off me before Amets gets jealous."

Laughing, Pasha leaned back and gave Amets a flirty grin. "I think he's more likely to get hard than jealous."

"Perhaps." Both of them turned and looked as the riders passed by. Neither knew a great deal about horses, but they knew quality when they saw it. All three of the beasts that passed by them were large, handsome creatures, and the three men were high quality, too. All were armed and armored, but even though Chavali didn't know much about that subject either, she knew these three men couldn't do much damage to the clan. Even Pasha, an eighteen year old dancer, knew how to fight.

"I wonder if they want something or are just passing by." Pasha dropped her doll and supplies where they wouldn't fall off and stood up to lean around the side of the wagon, using a handle mounted there to hold on.

Uninterested, Chavali returned her attention to the doll in her hands. "They want something."

"Do you have to flaunt how you know everything?"

"Yes." Without looking, Chavali felt quite certain Pasha was sticking her tongue out. Either that or rolling her eyes. She elected not to explain that her guess—which really was a guess—was based upon how the three men scanned them and struck her as very interested.

"They're slowing at Gotzon's wagon."

Chavali snorted a little. "You sound surprised. The one in front makes the choices of where we go. Obviously, to an Outsider, that driver would be the person in charge of the whole caravan. Forty-two wagons, all controlled by the whim of Gotzon."

Pasha giggled, kept watching. "The one in the back, he's kind of ugly."

"I didn't notice." This was both true and misleading. She wasn't paying attention to their looks, but was watching where their eyes went.

"He keeps turning back to watch behind. His face...he looks like he fell out of a tree the hard way."

Chavali snorted. "There's no rule that requires armed Outsiders on horses to be pretty."

"No, but there should be. If I have to watch them, they should be worth watching."

"Yes, the world should rearrange itself so Pasha always has something pleasant to look at, no matter where her eyes rest. Maybe you should just go jump Amets again. His little brother can drive well enough."

"I'm capable of waiting until we stop for the night."

"Is he?" Chavali chuckled and gestured towards Amets, who was staring at Pasha's behind now.

Pasha grinned, shook her bottom for him and waved. He was close enough to hear her if she shouted, but with the plodding of the horses, jangling of the harnesses, and creaking of the wagons, it wasn't truly worth the effort. Amets grinned back and lifted up an arm, flexed the muscles for Pasha. The woman sitting next to him, his mother, rolled her eyes and smacked him on the side, which made him cringe away, laughing.

Pasha giggled and returned to her seat and task, but it wasn't for long. The caravan pulled off to the side of the road early, only another half hour later. They had no specific destination or timetable, it wasn't as if it mattered much, the clan just usually kept going later into the day than this. As soon as the two sisters noticed they were leaving the road, they carefully put their dolls and supplies back into the box and hopped off the wagon to avoid being jostled even more because of the rougher ground.

Others did the same, they congregated in the center of what would be the camp. Normally, everyone would pitch in to dig out a fire pit, prepare dinner, and chase children while the wagons were settled and horses tended. Today, though, there were Outsiders among them. The three men hadn't left the caravan, and they sat on their horses off to the side, watching the activity and looking entirely uncertain what to do with themselves.

Chavali wasn't very good with these tasks, but she usually was able to at least help out a little, and doing so kept her from having to deal with Keino. Most often, she spent the time cutting things up or entertaining the children with a story. Right now, she stood in the midst of what must look like chaos, studying the Outsiders, getting a good look at them without bothering to hide she was doing so. When Papá and the other clan leaders were done getting the wagons in order, she'd learn what they wanted and why they were here, and wanted to have something of value to tell in return.

One was confident and interested, this was the pale one in the lead earlier. To her, it seemed like he wanted to offer to help, but at the same time, wasn't sure how that would be received. He had muscle mass, enough to fill out his fine plated armor and use that elegant looking sword belted to his waist. This was a man who came from money and had much privilege in his youth. Now he was entrusted with some kind of authority over others. At a guess, he was around the age of thirty. He watched the bustle of the camp without really seeing more than a group of people used to working together, no doubt.

The next was shorter and slimmer, a little less comfortable here, but she thought that had more to do with the particular surroundings than a lack of confidence. His armor was less obvious, mostly hidden under an outer layer of clothes, but she could see fine chain links at his wrists as he moved his hands, his stiff leather gloves not long enough to hide it, and the extra bulk was obvious from the size of his neck. His sword was less fancy, more functional, and he had a second one with it—a matched pair of them, one long and one short. This man wasn't as familiar with horses, but knew the basics of riding. He was reasonably attractive, but nothing Chavali found exceptionally noteworthy. He was probably about her age, and his eyes noticed her the most, stared right back at her.

Finally, the third man was…he was much larger than she thought. This man could probably reach up to the top of a wagon without stretching much, he must be near to seven feet tall. His horse was quite large as well, as it would need to be to hold a man of his size and in plated armor that, while in good condition, was not as ornate as the first man's. He was a soldier, she thought, or had been. He had that regimented, military air about him. Pasha called him 'ugly', but she thought that was excessive—his face had character in a way her younger sister wasn't attracted to. Of the three, though he was likely between the other two in age, he was the least certain of himself, probably new to whatever duty they upheld. His attention fell on the children—he clearly found them a joy to watch.

"Chavali!" Danel, a little boy of five, ran up and grabbed her skirt, tugged on it insistently. "Come tell me a story!" He smiled impishly when she looked down at him, and she grinned back. Outsiders could wait. When he darted away, she chased him. They wove through the men and women busy at their tasks. As she went, Chavali collected several other small children and wound up sitting on the ground with them, the youngest—Haizea—in her lap with her beloved doll clutched in her arms.

There was little she could do to get the very young to avoid touching her and she didn't bother trying. Their thoughts were disconnected and random anyway; she didn't feel like she was intruding on their privacy because they didn't understand the concept yet. Haizea was only three, and she thought about very simple things most of the time. It was fine for a little while. "Alright, little ones. I'll tell you a story you've never heard before."

As she expected, Papá came up by her side, crouched down next to her. Often, she was the one who had to say something first. He was that way with his wife, too, inclined to wait and let questions be asked rather than volunteer information or request opinions. Right now, though, she was busy and he knew it. "The one in front asked if they could share our camp tonight, for safety."

Chavali snorted. "As if anyone would attack men like that." The eight children she collected turned to look.

Papá nodded. "I expect they want something from us, but don't want to reveal it. We're allowing them to stay, though, because they offered payment in exchange for sharing the fire." The one thing a Blaukenev valued nearly as much as family was money. He scratched at the stubble on his chin a little. "We'd like you to entertain them. Keep them from causing trouble."

Her mouth curling into a smirk, Chavali nodded. "I'll take care of them."

Her father patted her arm approvingly, making sure it only touched her sleeve. "I'll see them to tending their horses, then send them to you." He didn't waste any more time, she watched him walk briskly over to the three men.

"Are you going to tell them the story, too?" Danel asked.

"Yes, I think so. In that case, we will practice Shappan. We do not speak the Blaukenev tongue in front of Outsiders." She shifted Haizea in her lap a little and got the rest to crowd in close. "So," she began in the Outsider language, speaking slowly and enunciating clearly, "today, we speak of grass. What is grass?" They all knew, of course, and delighted in showing her that they knew by ripping off handfuls of it and holding it up for her. This was really just to stall a little until the three men arrived, so they would hear the entire tale from start to end. By the time that was done, the children's mothers or fathers should be ready to have them back, and she could devote her full attention to the three men.

"Hm. What color is it?" The children chorused 'green!' gleefully and loudly. "Do we eat this?" An emphatic 'No' was tossed back to her. "Then what does?" Each child produced a different answer all at once, which made her laugh and go around to each one, getting their individual answers. None of them were wrong. By the time she coaxed Haizea to offer "bugs," the three men approached uncertainly. She waved to them to sit with the group. Biholtz also came over, bringing two more children and a cup of water for Chavali. The girl sat, too, providing a second pair of hands and eyes for what was now ten children.

"Gentlemen," Chavali said with a little nod of her head that made her beads click together. "Welcome to the Blaukenev camp. I am Chavali, at your service for the evening. Right now, I keep these ones out from under-foot. We speak of grass."

Pale Man took the lead, as expected. "Teryk, Eliot, Colby." He ges-tured to indicate that he was the first, Skinny was the second, Large Man the third. Eliot sat down, Teryk and Colby started removing their armor, making an effort to be quiet about it.

"It is nice to meet you," Chavali said politely. "Now, we get to the story." The children cheered, stopping any of the three men from object-ing. Colby, she noticed, was still watching the boys and girls with a kind of longing—he must wish to have children of his own. The other two were, so far as she could tell, less interested, just being polite. "Once upon a time," this was a cue for the listeners that the tale may not be completely true, "there were four goats. Their names were Iparre, Hegoa, Ekia, and Mendeba." The children knew these names already, but this was really all for the Outsiders.

"They were just like our goats," she waved vaguely off at the near-est members of the small herd the clan dragged along with them, now wan-dering around the campsite eating grass and old leaves. "Except they could talk. If our goats could talk, what do you think they would say?"

The answers were as expected, simple and cute, and displayed their varying difficulty with Shappan. "Grass yum", "Sleepy", "My feet ouch". Haizea didn't know the word she wanted to use and she whispered it to Chavali in the clan tongue, though she already knew what it was from touching the child. It was as good an answer as any other. "Haizea thinks they will ask each other for sex."

She noted the three men were surprised by that, to the point of being shocked. No matter. "I think you are all right, but these four goats did not say any of these things in this story. They walked across the land, surveying it and taking bites of the grass as they went. It was a good life, but quiet and empty. There were no baby goats, and they came across nothing else. Perhaps they walked in circles, but could not tell, for they were large circles.

"Iparre spoke after a time. 'I wish something new to eat', she said. 'Grass is boring. Let us turn to the north and seek new food.' All agreed that change would be good, but Hegoa shook her head. 'We should go south,' she said. Ekia suggested east, and Mendeba west. There they stood, stopped to argue, for they were a clan and did not wish to separate. It was just an argument at first, but Ekia decided to try to bully the others. He was the strongest, and his horns were longer and sharper than Mendeba's. They fought, like Fermin and Nikola with a cake in the middle." This made the children giggle. The two boys, teenage brothers, frequently squabbled in full view of the clan, over stupid things.

"The fight grew, and Ekia's horns came away from Iparre stained with her blood. This stopped the fight." She saw all of the children nodding, because this was how the clan was. Fights happened, but as soon as someone drew blood, it ended, either because the two combatants stopped

or because they were pulled apart. The three Outsiders listened thoughtfully, all of them. Perhaps she was revealing more about the clan than was
wise, but they could learn these things easily enough by just watching,
depending upon what happened while they were here.

"Ekia was ashamed, but also proved he was strongest. 'We will go
north,' he said, 'as Iparre wishes'. Mendeba and Hegoa agreed, feeling sorry
for Iparre that she must bear such a wound. They walked slowly now, letting Iparre have what rest they could while still moving. Her blood fell to
the ground in a line behind them, each drop reaching the earth and sinking
into it.

"Iparre did not heal. She stumbled and fell into the grass, unable to
go on. When the others stopped, they looked back and saw a line of purple
flowers standing among the grasses, showing the way they came. Ekia went
back to the nearest flower and bit it off, ate it. It was good, better than
grass. 'Stop,' Hegoa said to him, angry. 'Iparre is hurt, we must tend to her.
Without her, we are only three, not four. This is your fault, you must make
it right.'

"Ekia looked back and thought about it. Either he could eat the
flowers back the way they came, or he could tend to his clan. If he tended
to his clan, there would be no more purple flowers. What do you think he
did?"

Danel nodded definitively. "No clan is no happy." The rest of the
children nodded their heads in agreement.

"So it is," Chavali agreed. "Ekia turned away from the purple flowers to tend to Iparre's wounds. Because without clan, no one is whole."
Her eyes strayed to the rest of the camp and she saw she'd entertained the

children long enough. If the Outsiders weren't here, she would keep them longer, but she had her own duties to the clan to see to now. "Back to your parents." Lifting Haizea, she put the toddler on her feet and shooed them all off. Biholtz herded them in the right direction.

Chavali gestured for the three men to come closer now as she took a drink from her cup, because she wasn't going to get up and move for them. They glanced at each other, possibly all seeking approval for obeying her. She didn't want to give them a chance to ask a question first, so she started before they were settled again. "What brings you this way?"

Teryk made a vague little hand gesture. "Oh, the usual: orders and all." He said it casually, she thought he was being honest. "Why is your clan out here?"

She got half a smirk. "Where else would we be?"

Teryk gave her a look that wasn't quite a grin, but wasn't really anything else, either. It was tentative, hesitant. "This is a major undertaking, to move this many people around. There must be a reason you leave your homes to do it."

"The wagons are our homes." This was hardly a secret, there was no reason not to tell him. "We are nomads, from no country. To stay in one place is to stagnate, which is what we believe the Greatest Sin to be." This was not entirely true, of course, but for Outsiders, it was close enough.

"Interesting. I haven't heard that one before." Teryk nodded, accepting the notion. "I'm not much for the subject, really, it makes my head hurt to think about it overmuch." He was lying through his teeth, but Chavali had no need to call him on it. If he didn't want to share his beliefs, that was fine.

"Excuse me if this is a rude question," Eliot said, "but is that a real feather? And is it stuck there?" His voice was higher pitched than the other two, his curiosity was eating him.

This subject was one she had to tread carefully with, but she didn't let that show. "It is the mark of my position in the clan, and it is grafted to my skull." Ignoring most of the question was on purpose, of course.

"I haven't noticed anyone else with a feather like that." Colby gestured around to indicate the rest of the clan. "What position is that?"

"I am the clan Seer, which is largely a ceremonial title and has little to do with what you probably think of as a 'seer'. My duties are much closer to that of a lore keeper. As you have seen, I teach the children about the Sin and our clan, and similar such things, and also remind the adults of the stories from our past." This was both true and misleading, but these men would never know that. The most important part was that they needed not to know with certainty that she actually did sometimes deliver accurate prophecies.

The men shared another look. Chavali was quite certain they thought they found what they were looking for, which was interesting. "Why not call you 'Lore Keeper', then?" As Teryk spoke, he accepted a cup from Biholtz, who also gave one to Eliot, then Colby. Just a minute or so ago, Chavali noticed her mother speaking to the girl, this was likely intended to be helpful.

Chavali shrugged. "Tradition. Our clan was founded a long time ago, we have many such things that make little apparent sense but are still upheld. Without knowing where you are from—" This was a lie. She could tell from their accents that Teryk was from Mecalle and Eliot was from

Shappa. Colby had a more subtle accent. She needed to hear him speak more to guess his homeland. "—I feel comfortable saying your people do similar things."

Eliot snorted into his cup, Colby was also amused. Teryk grinned and nodded. "How long ago was the clan founded?"

Chavali waited a beat or two, making it look like she was trying to decide how much to really say. "Many hundreds of years."

"Really. That's quite a long time. I don't think any of the kingdoms are that old." This was why they were here, something related to this. He wanted to know something about the history of the clan, and she could tell he thought he was going to get it from her.

Chavali shrugged. "We have never been overly concerned with the ways people organize themselves into countries. Our way is to travel, always. Never two nights in a row in the same place without good reason. When we come upon a town, we sometimes stop and hold a carnival, so we can get money to buy things we are not equipped to make for ourselves. Metal working in particular is outside our capability, as it is difficult to transport a smithy. The clan has tried, of course, a few times, but these efforts end with disaster of one kind or another."

Without giving them a chance to interject another question or redirect the subject, she launched into a story that ought to distract them sufficiently. "One of these smiths was named Aitor, a man with the way of the tinker in his hands. He enjoyed the making of things, of new things especially. His best known creation was also his most ridiculous. You see, the clan had a problem." Strangely enough, all three of them listened to her with rapt attention, as if this was the most interesting thing they'd ever heard. She didn't expect this, and it perversely made her want to end the story without telling it. That was silly, though.

"Wagon wheels kept breaking. Every time they went over even a small bump, the wheels would break, one way or another. It might be the rim or a spoke, or some part of the axle. Although we had a mage then, who could fix these things, he spent too much of his time and power fixing them and worried greatly he would find himself in need of his magic for something more dire, only to be exhausted by fixing wagon wheels. As you can imagine, with this many wagons, and such fragility, much time and effort was spent fixing them."

As she took a breath to go on, Teryk gestured with his cup. "How many wagons were there then?"

Chavali paused and stared at him for a moment, mildly annoyed. She was not used to being interrupted. With young children, she would pause and get them to answer questions or participate, but that was not the same thing, and these were grown men. "We do not keep records of such things. It is fair to say the number was similar as now, forty-two." She was about to launch into the rest of the story, but Eliot now asked a question.

"The same? Hasn't your clan grown over time? Does it branch off every so often to keep from getting too big?" He seemed so earnest in his questions, the interest couldn't possibly be fake.

If they were trying to throw her off balance, it wasn't working. All they were really doing was making her more suspicious and hesitant. "I do not know this term 'branch off'."

Eliot looked at her like he wasn't sure he believed that, but shrugged. "Do people ever leave the clan? To go off on their own. Start a new clan or integrate into a city or something."

"No."

All three of them were surprised by this. Colby was the one who voiced it, though. "Never? Not even once?" He had a deep voice, that was no shock.

"No. Blaukenevs do not leave the clan. This is akin to death."

Colby opened his mouth, but shut it. Teryk instead asked, "You mean that you put to death anyone who tries, or there's something that makes your people want to stay?"

"We do not put our own to death, it is—" She had no desire at all to explain this coherently enough for them to understand. They were Outsiders. "-difficult to put in Shappan. Family is strong, deep. Clan is stronger, deeper." To emphasize the point, she tapped her chest with two fingers.

"But surely," Teryk prompted, "there's someone every once in a while who wants to leave rather than stay?"

Chavali shrugged, considering how to deflect a subject they apparently considered weird. She was aware that Outsiders didn't have the connection to their families and homes that the clan did, but didn't understand what that must be like. "We do not keep written records. Spoken only. Writings can be lost, burned, stolen."

All three men looked at her thoughtfully, she got the distinct impression they were hoping she would squirm under the scrutiny. Not likely. "I take it there are no stories about such misfits?"

"No, that is not a theme we pursue." There would be no taking back control of this conversation, not really, but Chavali didn't feel like she needed a rescue or distraction. One came anyway, in the form of Biholtz bringing food over. She gave Chavali a bowl first, then the guests, having carried them over on a tray. It was a thick stew, something they ate often; with so many people to feed, such meals were common. "I am curious if you find this familiar or strange." She gestured to her own bowl so they knew what she was talking about.

Teryk watched Biholtz, accepted his bowl and spoon with a nod of thanks. He seemed intrigued by something, but Chavali couldn't tell what. Though he opened his mouth to say something, Chavali gestured with her spoon towards his bowl and started to eat her own, watching him in the hopes these men would think she might consider them rude for not eating right away. Whether it was that or they were just hungry, the three men took the hint.

Colby was the one who made a noise of pleased surprise. "This is different, but I like it. What's in this?"

"I am not a cook, I know nothing of such things." It was now, as they each used their right hands to eat the stew, that she finally noticed the ring each of them wore on their middle finger. All three were exactly the same, a signet of some kind. The design wasn't one she recognized, though it tugged at a memory. Perhaps she'd seen one before, either directly or in someone's memories. After doing the fortune telling thing for so long and in every country multiple times, it was quite likely. Whatever the case, they were definitely all employed by or bonded to some singular entity.

"Is it alright to speak to the cooks? I'm just interested in the herbs you use. I noticed you have the gardens on top of some of the wagons, even grapevines and berry bushes, I'd love to find out more about your clan's cooking."

"Not everyone speaks Shappan well, but yes, feel free." Several people watched her and the Outsiders, they'd keep an eye on him. He clambered to his feet and walked away with a polite nod, bowl still in hand. She returned her attention to Teryk and Eliot, who both ate well enough to say they weren't only doing it out of politeness. "What sort of duty is it that brings you this way?"

Eliot snorted up some of his stew and coughed loudly to deal with that. Teryk reached over and thumped him on the back a little to help. "Nothing terribly interesting. Pay is pay, though. Nothing to really complain about."

All this tiptoeing around was starting to get annoying. They clearly wanted to know about the clan, specifically to know about the clan. "I see. May I take a closer look at your ring? You keep flashing it about, and I am interested in the design."

Teryk didn't want to do that, she could tell by the way he hesitated and grossly slowed down his chewing to give himself time to think. "It's, ah, not really anything worth wasting time on." He seemed to realize this was a stupid excuse on his own and offered her his hand, which she took to peer at the design.

Just take a look and forget about it, because it's nothing. Come on, don't linger over it or think about it too much.

Naturally, the thoughts the spirits pulled out of his mind made her want to belabor the point, dawdle on the subject. "Is this the mark of the person to whom you owe your duty?"

"Yes." *Eldrack is going to kill me if you—* That was all she got before he pulled his hand back and returned to eating. "He's a good man, we serve him out of loyalty."

Teryk spoke the truth, but Eliot didn't fully agree with him. Interesting. Manufacturing another reason to touch one of them would be difficult, which was a shame. Talking would have to do. She nodded her understanding. Could she coax out something about this Eldrack person? Perhaps. "I do not recognize the symbol. Where is he located, this man who commands your respect?"

"Shappa." Teryk's curt reply made her raise her eyebrows a little. Touchy subject, that. He didn't like working for someone with authority in Shappa, it sounded like.

"Intriguing that you should find us in Tila, then." She said this just because she wanted to watch them react. Both focused on their food, telling her they weren't quite prepared to answer such a question.

It took Teryk about a minute to come up with something else to say. "This is really good. I hope the cooks will take Colby's interest as thanks from us all, or should we each make the effort to say something individually?"

So, they really did come here to find the clan. That was the duty they pursued, not something else. "They will not be offended by passing strangers not taking the time to thank them personally for being allowed to share our meal."

Colby returned without his bowl, a cheerful smile on his face. It was a strange expression for him. He seemed better suited to stoicism, or perhaps staring out over something in satisfaction. Like a battlefield. "I have a few new recipes to try."

Chavali set her empty bowl and spoon aside and watched Colby, interested to know if he'd reveal anything the other two hadn't. "I am surprised they were willing to part with their secrets for you."

Chuckling a little, Colby shook his head. "I just asked what the herbs were. Your clan has some unusual combinations that make interesting results."

She nodded like this was a clever observation, but didn't want to pursue the subject. There was no reason to reinforce for them how little the clan actually mingled with Outsiders. "Are you on your way back to Shappa now, or do you have business in North Cascain?"

Teryk set his bowl aside, also. "We're going home to Shappa, yes. Is that where the clan is headed?"

Chavali shrugged noncommittally. "Possibly. I do not make such decisions. We may turn east because of bad weather or a good omen, or any number of reasons. We follow no particular schedule, and the decision of where to go is made by our clan leaders, usually in the morning."

Colby blinked at her. "You mean you don't have any kind of set path? You don't go back to the same places all the time?" The more he spoke, the more certain she was of his country of origin: Grippa.

"This would be just a different kind of stagnation. We go where the whim takes us. There have been times when we have found a way impassable and had to turn around and find another path. It happens. We always know where we are, of course, we have maps, but the destination is not the goal, it is the journey itself which matters."

"Ah." Eliot gave Colby a somewhat disapproving look, but it didn't shut him up. "And what has your journey taught you?"

"That is a very personal question." Chavali smirked, mostly because Colby looked embarrassed for asking it, for not realizing it was.

"Oh, ah, well. I..."

Teryk cleared his throat delicately. "He meant more from the perspective of the entire clan, I think."

"Yes," Colby nodded with some relief, "that's what I meant. I'm sorry for any offense."

If only she could get Colby by himself, without the other two around to keep him in check. "None is taken. I would need a rather long time to relate all the tales which speak of what the clan has learned in our many generations. And," she smirked, "you would all need to not interrupt me as I tell them. I suspect, however, your master will want you back before then."

"Oh, no, he—"

Eliot nudged Colby in the ribs to cut him off. "He isn't expecting us back yet. We're ahead of schedule."

"Maybe," Teryk suggested, "we can ride along with your clan for the day tomorrow, and you can regale us with tales as we go?"

"My stories are not free, of course, and we have no place for strange men inside our wagons, but I could certainly tell them to one of you as you ride along tomorrow. We place no claim upon the road itself." If they were willing to pay, the clan leaders would agree to this. "Colby's horse is large enough I could probably ride with him for a while to make sure my words are heard properly."

Colby nodded earnestly, looked to Teryk. "She's small enough, Karias can handle it. I doubt either of your mounts can."

Chavali stifled down a grin of victory. That was a strange name for a horse, but something to puzzle over later. "We could carry some of your gear to lighten the load on your mount perhaps, as a show of good faith. Some of your possessions for the clan Seer. Not a fair trade by any measure, but satisfactory for a single day." She'd need to wear pants tomorrow, something to remember. Although she didn't have much experience riding, she knew that much.

Teryk wasn't very happy about this, but tried to hide it. "What would you charge for that?"

"Negotiate with my father," she gestured off towards the fire without looking, knowing he'd be over there someplace, probably watching her. "If he agrees, then I agree."

Teryk's eyes followed her gesture and frowned. None of the three of them noticed her make a little hand signal, and so they were all a little surprised when Papá stood up and ambled over. Teryk stood up and met the man partway, they spoke quietly enough Chavali couldn't overhear. She didn't watch them anyway, she watched Eliot and Colby. The former was conflicted about this idea, the latter pleased.

"Either way," Chavali said, distracting both of them from the negotiation. "I am still here right now. May I ask your indulgence to allow me to practice my trade on you?"

"I beg your pardon?" Eliot blinked several times, refocusing on her.

"Fortune teller. It is a skill as much as anything else. You seem to me to be skeptics, which I encounter infrequently, and I would appreciate the opportunity to try to impress you."

"Oh." Eliot was put off by the idea, not interested. She could tell before he refused. "I, ah, no, thank you."

Colby, on the other hand, was amused. "Sure, that's fine. How do you do it?"

Another victory, thanks to Colby. Chavali liked this man, in the same way she liked a rabbit who jumped into the snare on purpose so she could have dinner. Shifting to get a little closer, she reached for him. "Give me your hand."

"Do you read the lines?" He obliged, letting her take it. *This is silly, but I like the feel of your skin. Your hands are very smooth.*

"No." His hands were so much larger than hers, she wriggled a little closer to use both of hers for his one. "Come, ask something, anything. Even a silly question."

She wants me to ask her something silly, so I can't think of anything. Along with his thoughts, there was something else in his mind, a queer second thread, one she didn't know what to make of. It was like...but that made no sense. Perhaps he merely had some odd ability to detach himself, or some trauma that separated his mind into parts, something along those lines. Yes, that made sense. He must have some horrible, dark secret kept hidden away to protect himself from it. *Maybe a trick question, like whether I like beets or not? She couldn't possibly know that I do.* "Um, do I like beets?"

Chavali gave him a look to show him exactly how ridiculous that kind of question was, making sure to wait until it actually came out of his mouth. "I have only two choices for this kind of question, Colby, it is not a good question. But yes, you do." He was surprised she guessed right, but a glance over at Eliot showed he thought this was stupid. "People come to me for advice, more or less. They wish for the guidance of mysterious forces because they do not like the answers they can come up with on their own. Do you have any matters you wish assistance with resolving, or deciding?"

He immediately thought of things she didn't understand. They went by so quickly she couldn't get a good grasp on them. There was a fire, half-breed children were involved, his horse was not a horse but still a horse, an oath given, a life stolen, an attractive blonde woman with lips he needed to forget but couldn't. There was more, much more, but she couldn't handle it all, couldn't sort it all. Letting go with a sharp intake of breath, she backed away from him, got to her feet, and walked—nearly ran —away to get some space. She didn't stop until she was at the outer edge of the wagons, then she leaned against the nearest one rubbing her face.

"Chavali?" Papá followed her. She looked and saw Teryk was just behind him, concerned. Her father followed her eyes and flicked a hand to shoo the man away. "Go, leave her be," he snapped. Teryk backed off, his hands up in surrender. With the Outsider gone, he used the clan's tongue. "What happened?"

By now, she had a chance to take a few deep breaths and calm down. "There were things in his mind, Papá," she muttered. "They're definitely here to see us. Something happened to the big one, he...I don't know, it makes no sense, and it was— His own mind recoils from it, but embraces it at the same time. It's hard to explain, but I think," she paused, because the obvious explanation made no sense. As the pause stretched out, he looked at her expectantly. "I don't know."

Papá crossed his arms and nodded. "Go to bed, then. You're more important than knowing what they're up to. They'll go in the morning whether they want to or not. When they're gone, we'll discuss them more."

Wishing he would hug her, she nodded and sighed while hugging herself. "How much did he offer for my services?"

"Not enough for this. Some things aren't worth it." It cost him nothing to say that, but she could tell he was disappointed to be losing out on what seemed like easy money. Truth be told, so was she.

Chapter 6

As soon as Teryk, Eliot, and Colby left them the next morning, the caravan turned west, toward the mountains. The elders changed their intended course to be on the safe side. The clan had used a pass there many times before. In the winter, it turned treacherous with snow and ice. Late summer, though, held no particular dangers. Shappa lay on the other side. If those three men or their employer decided to look for the clan, they'd be found eventually. Chavali needed only a week or two to sort herself out, which also give the clan enough time to prepare for the possibility they would come back, either with or without reinforcements.

Nothing new had happened, of course. The clan had fought off angry townspeople before and would again. With this potential active threat, though, weapons stayed closer to hand and the elders steered farther from civilization. For a little while, anyway. Living like this for an extended time didn't appeal to anyone, and Chavali really only needed a few days to push it all away, to force it to leave her alone. Examining it all held no appeal for her, she just wanted it to recede into the background with all the rest of the things she saw in other people's minds.

This particular pass put them near to one of the Creator's Towers, and the town nearby was sizable because of it. To throw off the shadows chasing them, the clan set up their carnival just outside it, acting as if nothing changed, nothing strange happened. Keino, who hadn't approached her at all since the morning she was attacked, didn't look at her while he set up her table and rolled her stumps into place. She had nothing to say to him, either. If only the silence wasn't tense and strained, heavy with anticipation of him breaking it unpleasantly, she might be put in a good mood by it.

It was far from gone, his interest in her. As he worked, straightening and arranging, he stole glances at her. Perhaps, she thought, he figured if he left her alone, she would eventually seek his attentions out because of withdrawal. Indeed, perhaps she would, if only because that meant coming to him on her own terms. When he left the tent, it was with a long and longing look back at her, then he was gone. Yes, someday, she would return it. When he actually deserved it.

The day passed slowly. She sat in her tent with a smooth red-brown stone and tools occupying her hands for most of it. Making and maintaining her baubles took work, a kind she couldn't do on a bouncing wagon. The times like this when no one was bothering her, that was when she pursued this work. The spirits directed her hands, sculpting the shape, then carving out its rune with a scraping tool. The finishing touch would be to wash the new carving with a staining ink, but she hadn't gotten that far by the time her stomach informed her they would be shutting down the carnival soon.

Keino poked his head into the tent as she slipped the unfinished stone into her pouch and stood up, stretching her arms above her head. His eyes took in the sight of her, but he sounded brusque and businesslike when he spoke. "There's one last customer tonight, I told him you were ready to stop for the day, but he paid double."

She rolled her shoulders and nodded. There was no good reason to turn down twice her price, especially given how light the day's take was. "It's fine. Give me a minute, then let him in." Shaking out her fingers and bending over to touch her toes was enough stretching for now and she sat back down. It took her another few moments to exert her possession over her table and affix her usual airy yet mysterious seer expression on her face.

About half a minute later, a young man—he was probably in his early twenties—entered the tent confidently. His light brown hair was pulled back into a neat tail and he had a slim, friendly looking face with light colored eyes, probably blue. Pasha would call him an attractive man— Chavali would agree—and he seemed perfectly at ease and comfortable as he seated himself across from her.

"Good evening," he said smoothly, meeting her eyes with an assured smile. "I have a business venture that my friends and I are about to embark on. I would like you to look into my future and tell me if we will be successful and at what cost."

This was not the usual sort of person Chavali saw in her tent. He felt off. People like him didn't seek out people like her. She saw the desperate, the lonely, the deluded, the foolish. This man was none of those things, and that he was here bothered her. "I will tell you what I can, but the future is fluid, not a set path. I am more adept with the past and the present, as they are already set and unchangeable." Though he held out his hand already, she hesitated to offer hers.

"Ah," the man said with a knowing smile. "But it is our choices and situations in the past that help shape our decisions in the present which will ultimately lead to our future. So, I believe you capable, else I would not trouble you." Still his hand lay there on the table, demanding her compliance.

Double the fee, she reminded herself. He paid double for this, and she did what was best for the clan so long as it didn't harm anyone. That he made her uncomfortable wasn't enough for her to refuse and have him be paid back. When she told Papá why she threw him out of her tent, she needed a better reason than 'he was all wrong'. To get that better reason, she would have to see what was in his head.

Layered callouses, the sign of a man who worked all his life, covered warm, dry hands. Small scars ran over his wrist, disappearing into his sleeve. She took it tentatively. He let her control the grip and didn't try to latch on or pull her closer. Normally, the instant she made contact, the spirits swarmed the other person and fed her something: coherent thoughts, images, emotions, or bursts of fuzzy thought.

He had no thoughts. His mind felt as blank as a stone. She stared, confused, and waited until she realized he fooled her somehow. Instead of blank, his mind held an overwhelming ocean of steadfast calm. Under the surface, she caught a thread of apprehensive excitement, anticipation of both the best and the worst.

When she glanced up from her hand to his face, she was disturbed to find him staring at her, at her eyes, not hiding an intense interest she couldn't sense from his thoughts. Like this, he put her in mind of a predator watching its prey, waiting for her to do something that would reveal the best way to strike. It was wrong, so very, very wrong. She should have trusted her instincts in the first place, but now she had a reason to toss him.

"Get out," she snapped, yanking on her hand. "Let go of me." A rising tide of panic churned in her belly when his fingers curled around her wrist and refused to let go.

For a moment, while his eyes flicked over her, she almost thought he would just toss her hand away and leave her be. "I don't think so." His voice had gone cold and hard. "I'm a paying customer and you *will* tell me what I want to know." His eyes went flat and he twisted her hand sharply, forcing her up off her seat and halfway over the table.

She wanted to scream, but couldn't find her voice enough to do more than whimper as he held her arm in a vise-like grip at an odd angle, threatening to break her wrist. He was strong enough to do that. He could snap it like a stick if he wanted to, and he used that grip to wrench her to her feet and pull her close to him. She froze when he twisted her arm behind her back and held her close, certain he would do something much worse if she cried out.

Something threaded through her mind, a whisper making promises she couldn't comprehend but knew she didn't want. Where it touched, velvet brushing over her and forcing her breath out in tiny gasps, it left behind an oily film. It was a seeping, oozing stain on her mind that pushed away coherence and demanded obedience.

"So that's how it works," he murmured. She heard the cruel smile in his voice, felt his poisoned breath on her neck. "Which means that I will do this." A sudden sharp stab into her mind made her open her mouth to scream, but only a harsh, ragged breath came out. Purple slid across her vision like it always did when the spirits forced a prophecy on her. The only thing she could do was to save her resolve to scream for Keino when it ended. Terrified of the fact that he could force it to happen, she wanted to struggle but couldn't. The spirits held her rigid, like they always did.

"The rose fills, the blood spills, the plan fulfills, the hand kills. The toll is taken twice and thrice. For success, that is the price."

He couldn't know what would happen next. She seized the opportunity afforded by the moment before he realized it had ended and screamed for Keino. Startled by her shrill shriek, he pushed her away. She crumpled to the ground as the pain hit her. Determined, she tried to crawl away, but couldn't manage much when all she wanted to do was to curl up into a ball.

Behind him, Keino burst through the tent opening, taking in the situation quickly and making Chavali look back with relief. "I think it's time for you to leave," he growled, reaching out toward the stranger. The man didn't move, his eyes intent on the fortune teller at his feet. Keino grabbed him, anger evident in his every fiber. The stranger flared his nostrils, and Chavali felt that something happened, though she couldn't say what until Keino's eyes widened in horror and he froze as still as a statue. Icy panic gripped her as she understood this man could kill or worse with nothing more than a thought.

"The Order of the Strong Arm has come for you, Chavali. You have something we want, something we need. We will take it from you and then, if you are very, very lucky, we will kill you." Outside, she could hear grunts, screams, cries, clangs of metal on metal. "That would be my men and, as you know, we will succeed in tonight's raid. I will lose more than I suspected, but you and yours will fall to me. No one can save you, Chavali—especially not yourself."

Her own mouth just told her that she wasn't going to get away from him. It didn't matter in the slightest what she did or didn't do, because he was going to get what he wanted. He reached down and laid just a finger on her, wracking her body with more agony. From the brief contact, she knew he meant it to be just enough to make her too weak to fight back, too weak to do anything but lie there.

But the future was fluid. Chavali believed everyone had free will and the spirits could only tell most likely outcome based upon established patterns of the world and everyone acting according to their natures. Though casual observation wouldn't reveal it, all the men and women of her clan, and many of the older children, had plenty of experience and skill with fighting. They would fight back against attackers with the weapons always kept close at hand during the carnivals. The spirits knew this and could guess how many it would take to overwhelm the clan.

Though the pain made thinking difficult, Chavali concentrated on what she could do that the spirits would never expect. His words ran through her mind—*if you are very, very lucky, we will kill you*—twice, then three times, and she knew the answer, even if she didn't like it. Better to choose your own fate than to be a slave to someone else's choice.

For show, because it suited her costume, she kept a small knife belted at her waist. It was nothing more than a sharp eating knife and of no threat to anyone, especially in her untrained hands. She steeled herself with the thought that defying him in death would be better than serving him in agony. The spirits knew she wanted to live, so this path offered the only option to defeat this despicable man. Hand shaking, blood steadily flowing from her nose and eyes and ears, she grabbed that little knife and pulled it out of its little sheath.

"Cute," he sneered over her, apparently convinced she meant to keep trying to fight back. Good. It made him take a step back to show how little she would accomplish with that tiny blade.

He wasn't the one she meant to use it on. If only she could squeeze her eyes shut to do this. But then she might miss, and there would be only one chance to get this right. Clenching her jaw, she moved as quickly as she could manage and stabbed it through her own wrist. It hurt, but not nearly so much as what was in her head. Yanking the blade back out was likely the last thing she'd ever do. She hoped it would be, fervently.

The man still chuckled behind her until he saw the blade slick with her blood. "No," he finally said after a long pause, the one word faint and shocked. Then he rushed to crouch down beside her and grabbed her wrist, her blood pumping out in gushing bursts over his hands, spraying them scarlet. "No," he repeated, firmly. "You can't die yet," he said, sounding angry and confused and stunned and horrified.

She didn't really care. What mattered was that he didn't heal her. He couldn't heal her. She knew that because his mind told her so. Drunk from the blood loss already, she giggled at his thoughts. He'd planned this to the last detail. He knew exactly how much the human body could take before it shut down, and couldn't understand how she managed to defy him. And yet, she did.

He didn't count on her being difficult. The entire clan would have laughed in his face if they knew that had been his mistake.

Chapter 7

There was nothing she could do. Railan crouched in the shadow of a small stand of trees, her fingers fiddling with her unlit pipe, her horse lying in the grass behind her. The only reason the beast remained content had to be the plentiful food all around its head, because the sounds here were extremely unpleasant. By the time she got here, there was very little fighting still going on, mostly just screaming. If she arrived a little sooner, maybe she could have evened the odds some. That she was too late to do anything other than not get herself killed was galling.

Why someone came to slaughter the clan was a mystery, especially that it should happen now. Did the three Fallen sent to investigate it lead someone else to them, or was it coincidence? The idea made her snort softly. As if anything ever happened by chance around Fallen or in their wake. Eldrack signed the death warrant for these people by sending Fallen to talk to them, whether he would admit it or not.

The screaming wasn't stopping, but was being produced by fewer and fewer voices. It was more like wailing, really, the sound of abject despair. If she was one of the last ones left alive while everyone she knew and loved was slain all around her, she would probably make that noise, too. The worst part was how much of this she could see. Her hiding spot gave her a great view in through the space where their camp was open on one side.

One of the men was in a frothing rage, covered with blood from head to toe as he cut through these people. The rest were more perfunctory about the whole thing, just doing their job, but that one man, he had pure venomous hate for this clan. He screeched at them, cut heads off, stabbed children, she even saw him break a baby in two without batting an eye.

Suddenly, he stopped, one hand gripping the hair of a girl so harshly she couldn't look anywhere but the sky She couldn't be more than twelve or so. His other hand held his sword ready to plunge into her chest, but he didn't do it. Instead, he stood there like that, the girl panting and terrified, him staring down at her. Lowering his sword, he shoved her at some of his men instead and barked some orders. Railan was too far away to hear most of it, but she made out a few words, enough to guess he meant to take this one with them as a prisoner.

Poor girl, nothing good would happen to her. There was still nothing Railan could do here, not until they finished and left. She wanted to charge out there and save that girl or kill them both trying, but she would never learn anything if she was dead, and there were still too many of those men for her skills. Had she really only dropped down behind these trees a few minutes ago? It felt like so much longer.

They started burning things. Those beautiful wagons—probably crafted by masters and decorated lovingly over the years—were being destroyed, and who knew why. The deranged man mounted up and watched the camp put to the torch, then watched while the girl, bound and gagged, was thrown over a horse and tied there. It looked like they were taking another two people along with her, smaller ones that were also tied up.

Hopes of the three prisoners being taken separately from the main group were dashed when they all mounted up and moved out together. The attackers lost several of their own, she could tell by how many of their horses were riderless now. At least these people went down fighting and took two dozen or so with them. She whispered a prayer for the Creator to watch over those three kids and waited in the gathering darkness for the riders to be gone without a doubt.

The burning wagons meant it wasn't truly dark, of course. Several minutes after the sounds of their hoof beats ended, she hurried over, hoping against hope there would be something worth salvaging, something that would actually answer questions. Right now, the most critical question seemed to be who did this and why, but there were others, less pressing, that a member of the clan who wasn't quite dead might be able to answer. Some of their possessions might also tell enough of a story to reveal a piece of the puzzle.

Thanks to that gap in the wagons, she was able to lope right into the ring of fire and start looking around. Most of the bodies were too close to flames to be worth checking, and the rest were quite obviously dead. Still, she trotted through the camp and found herself around the back of the center ring of tents—none of them were on fire yet, but with the breeze, they soon would be. Curiously, one of those tents was ripped apart, half of it thrown aside and the other half partially covering an intriguing wooden table.

The table was lacquered and painted with runes, ones she didn't recognize. It was small, the kind for intimate meals between two people. In here, there was a man's body, no real violence done to him. She stooped and checked for a pulse, but his eyes were stuck wide open in horrified shock. From there, she noticed a woman's arm with pink polish on the nails, lying on the ground, the rest of her hopefully under the tent cloth.

Pulling it up, she did find the owner of the hand, lying in plenty of her own blood. It came from her eyes, her nose, her mouth, even her ears, and from a sizable hole in one wrist where she'd been stabbed through. It was a strange way to die in the center of all this. What really caught her eye was the curled pink feather growing out of the woman's forehead, marking her as that lore keeper Teryk indicated in his report.

Railan brushed the feather, unable to prevent herself from doing it. The act made her shiver for no reason she could fathom. Examining it with her own mind was tempting, but she was right in the middle of an uncontrolled fire right now. Instead, she grabbed the whole woman under her arms and dragged her out of it before the flames could take the corpse. She hauled the body over to her horse and went back, just in case there was anything else useful to be taken.

Some of the bodies were definitely not from the clan, and she found a few not yet burning to check over. Any clue they could offer about who did this would help. Three different men hadn't been killed too messily, she checked their pockets and admired the clan's handiwork. These kills were swift and clean, the work of people who knew what they were doing, though she didn't know enough to say much else about it.

Each of the men had a handful of coins, that wasn't surprising. One had a ring that might be a wedding band. She took all of that—she wasn't above looting corpses, especially these corpses. When she found nothing to otherwise identify any of them, she started looking for a mark of some kind. It was an effort to pull the chainmail armor off, but she managed it, coughing a little from the flames all around her when she was done. Her time was well spent, as it turned out. He had an unfamiliar tattoo on his shoulder, one she pulled out a scrap of paper and pen to copy.

Now she knew where to look, she found the same mark on the other two, which was good enough to say it meant something. Someone would recognize it, and then it would just be a matter of finding the right person to bribe, threaten, or persuade into divulging what it meant. That handled, she paced through and picked up a few things tossed about and still intact. Too bad she couldn't take that table, it looked like a lot of work went into its decoration.

A handful of mementos wasn't much, but at least this woman might have a few things from her home whenever she got around to caring about such things again. With the woman's corpse slung over her saddle, she started leading the horse back. Her pipe quickly found its way to her mouth. She invoked the small enchantment to make it light up and savored the sweet smoke that filled her senses. It was a way to distance herself from what she just sat through, from the knowledge she just watched helplessly while a unique culture was destroyed. In a little while, she'd jog, but for now, she needed to walk.

It was a little surprising how close to the Fallen's Tower they were here. Eldrack suggested three places to look for the traveling clan, and she picked this one first, just because it seemed so unlikely to be where they'd go. No one went through the mountains. Why bother? Considering the cost of the supplies it would take to get from one side to the other, it was cheaper and faster to use the Creator's Towers. Yet, they did. Those wagons trundled right through one of the passes. Then again, they did charge extra for wagons and horses, maybe it wasn't that great a deal for the clan. Come to think of it, they might not routinely have that much coinage among them.

Regardless, it was only a day's walk from here to the Fallen's Tower. As she went, puffing every so often on her pipe, she wondered about the feather, about the beads, about this woman's injuries, about the attack itself. "You're a mystery, Seer Chavali, that's what you are. The focal point for many mysteries, in fact. Makes you a prime candidate for the Fallen. Just hope you're up to it."

She kept off the road, not wanting to attract any attention to the fact she was hauling a corpse around, especially this particular one. Come nightfall, she found herself a place to camp and stared at the body for a while. Good thing it wasn't terribly warm. The body was rigid now, stuck how it was hung over the horse. That might pass by morning, it might not. How much she knew about such things bothered her a little, but part of her job was handling them, picking them up and hauling them home.

By morning, the skin was that awful purplish-blue color of death. Railan threw a blanket over the still stiff body. No sense parading her through town when she got there. There was always someone who would gawk, so she did what she could to give the people she brought in some small amount of dignity. A few hours later, she had to find the road, and around noon, she plodded into the small farming village of Cloverdale. It looked the same as it always did in late summer: full of people working together to get the first part of the harvest in. Anyone coming through here had to assume most of it was to be sold elsewhere, but in reality, whatever wasn't needed by the village went to support the Fallen.

The stables was a sizable building, built to accommodate many more beasts than this small town would ever need, and not just horses. The hard part here was getting the body where it needed to be without having to be the one hauling it, but there were a couple of strapping male Fallen in the stables who took it off her hands, leaving her free to handle the horse, then go straight to Eldrack.

Whenever she needed him, he always seemed to appear someplace nearby, never actually looking for her, or aware she wanted something from him. It was kind of queer, but the one time she asked about it, he just smiled politely and changed the subject. And there he was, in the tavern. He never came up to the tavern that she knew of, yet he sat there, sipping at a cup of something and chatting with the barmaid. The place was strangely deserted, probably because the Administrator was here. Anyone just coming up to relax for a little while would walk right on outside to get some fresh air instead.

"Fancy meeting you here," she said as she sat down at the bar beside him. Uninterested in staying here for long, she waved the barmaid off and made a subtle gesture to ask her to not stay close.

Eldrack smiled at her. "I saw two just come through with an unexpected package."

"The clan was attacked. They were pretty thorough. That was the one you wanted me to talk to, the lore keeper woman."

"Ah." He sighed and sipped at his cup. "It never really ends."

"There's more. The attackers took some kids, three I think. Hard to say if all three will still be alive by nightfall, but he took them for a reason." She described the particular, peculiar way the man changed his mind about killing them.

Frowning, he sighed again, stared into his cup. "He may have just decided to take toys."

She fished in her pocket and pulled out the paper with her drawing. "Maybe. But, just in case, I found this on some of the corpses of his own men he left behind. A tattoo."

He took it, examined it. "I don't recognize it, but that doesn't mean anything." The paper went into his pocket.

"Yeah, that's how I felt about it."

"Was it bad?"

"I've never seen anyone kill that viciously before. How twisted do you have to be to—" Eldrack didn't need to hear about that. She sighed. "I didn't have any nightmares last night, but it's probably only because I didn't sleep much."

Eldrack downed the last of his drink and set it gently on the bar. "You know where to find Healer Ellen. It sounds like I have work to do." Standing up, he left a silver piece on the bar even though he didn't have to.

"Yeah." She watched him take a step away before remembering something. "Oh, I should say there's something funny about the feather, but I didn't take the time to really look it over."

He paused, considered that, then nodded. "I'm not surprised. Thank you, Railan."

Chapter 8

Chavali awoke to pain. That was how she knew she wasn't dead. Her wrist was pure agony. Her head was worse, so bad it was hard to think. She wanted to reach up to cradle her head, wanted to curl up in a ball, but couldn't. Half-remembered snatches of queer nightmares lingered in her mind, but they faded to at least give her some kind of relief. Her throat was raw, her eyes clenched shut so hard tears leaked from the corners.

"Ssh," a soothing female voice whispered. "The pain will fade, I promise."

A hand touched her brow, gently, tentatively, but it felt like a spike was shoved into her head. Somehow, it hurt so much more for that woman's thoughts to press on her, like she was rubbed raw and these thoughts were sandpaper. She tried to scream, but it came out as a hoarse cry. The hurt it put on her throat was so minimal compared to her head it barely registered, but it certainly didn't help, either. The hand was yanked away, thankfully.

"I'm sorry," the woman said, but Chavali didn't care. "Try to sleep."

That seemed impossible, but it was a strange thing for her captors to say, making her wonder just where she was. Cracking her eyes open proved to be a very bad idea, as there was too much light for her to handle right now. She whimpered and shut them again quickly. Something still held her, kept her from curling up. She struggled against it, but was too weak to manage anything. Not that there was any point to trying. No doubt, she was out long enough she could be secured quite thoroughly. And now, she was trapped.

The only thing left to her was tears. She couldn't scream, couldn't get away, could only hope to be killed swiftly. Except she was sure she died. Her memory was very clear: she stabbed herself, he had no way to save her, she bled out. As she lost consciousness, she felt a rush of something pulling her down, then a strange swirl of things she couldn't make sense of. Voices, she remembered there were a lot of voices—many different ones all screaming and moaning and wailing. Something else; she flailed to hold onto the memory, but it danced out of her reach.

"Sleep, Chavali, just sleep. Things will make more sense when you wake up." The woman's voice was still soft and soothing.

She wanted to say something rude, but knew her throat hurt too much. Chavali tried to relax through the pain, settled into the breathing exercises she used when they were first trying to find the right combination of things to ease the spirits. It didn't diminish the pain, not even a little, but it did give her some peace, and she slept.

It was much later when she awoke again, the pain gone. She still couldn't move much, but her head was clear. Opening her eyes cautiously, she found the light much dimmer than before. The space she lay in was a small room, not terribly different from the inside of a wagon, aside from being made of stone and devoid of personal items. The bed was actually a cot and she was strapped down to it, a sheet covering her body from about the neck down. Next to the cot, a small table sat with a pile of folded dark cloth on it. A wooden folding chair rested against the wall on the other side of the bed. The door stood ajar, just enough so she could tell it was unlocked and unlatched.

Where the light came from was a mystery, she couldn't see any source for it. More importantly, though, she was thirsty and couldn't use her hands. It was peculiar she'd been allowed to rest until the pain was gone. Maybe she screamed so much they killed her and this was actually some kind of afterlife.

"Hello?" Her voice was a rough croak, harsh and cracking.

A young woman stuck her head in through the door, she wasn't part of the clan. Her skin was too pink, her hair too light, her clothes too plain and utilitarian. No Blaukenev would be caught dead in something so unflattering as that dress. Except, perhaps, for the one lying on the cot right now, but she wore nothing save the sheet covering her still. The girl brought in a tray with a cup and covered plate on it, her expression uncertain. Chavali guessed she must be no older than twenty at the most. Her hair was tucked under some kind of floppy hat thing, it looked silly.

The girl brought the tray over and set it on the table. "Hello." The voice was familiar, the one Chavali heard before, making promises. As it turned out, she was right, making Chavali disposed to trust her, at least somewhat. "I'm Healer Kelly."

Delightful. "Am I a prisoner here, Healer Kelly?" She whispered, though this hurt at least as much as speaking aloud.

"Oh," Kelly flushed a little and bent to start undoing the straps. "No, not at all. We were concerned you might hurt yourself when you first woke up."

Considering the last thing she did, this seemed a reasonable concern. In a manner of speaking. "Where am I?"

"Administrator Eldrack will answer your questions, but after you've eaten and dressed." Kelly paused in her efforts to undo the straps, pointed to the dark cloth. "It's not much, but it'll serve you well enough until you can get regular things to wear. As soon as I leave here, I'll go fetch him for you, but he's a busy man, it may be a little while."

Chavali sat up as soon as she was able, lifted her hands and turned them over. Her left wrist had a scar on both sides, where the knife went through. Somehow, this small thing eased her mind a great deal. All of that happened, it wasn't her imagination or a dream. She was not going mad. Oh, spirits, all of that happened. A shudder ran down her spine, she rubbed her face. There was no way to wipe off that taint, though. Her hands covered her face while she tried to push away that feeling, but it was too stubborn for now.

"Whatever happened, I'm sure time will make it easier to bear." Chavali looked up and thought about laughing in the girl's face, but Kelly held out a cup of liquid for her and had a sympathetic smile. "Whenever you're ready to talk about it, I'll listen."

Taking the cup carefully to avoid touching Kelly's hand, Chavali wasn't sure how to respond. So far, Kelly had been nice and pleasant, but she remained an Outsider. Chavali settled on shaking her head and sipping at what turned out to be plain, cool water. It felt like exactly what she needed right now, the perfect thing for her throat. She drained the cup quickly, surprised at how thirsty she suddenly was. Her stomach, too, woke with this, and growled and gurgled.

Without needing to be asked, Kelly moved the tray over and pulled the cover off. It could have been a pile of animal feed and she would still have eaten it with relish. Instead, it was fresh bread, some kind of chunky soup, cheese, apple, other things she wasn't familiar with. Despite her usually small appetite, she devoured everything, hardly bothering to taste or savor any of it. Her belly seemed to be a vast, yawning pit in need of filling.

Kelly left her to eat alone. Chavali set the tray aside when she was done with it and picked up the dark cloth. It was soft, but turned out to be a very plain shirt and pants. Still, something was better than nothing and she shrugged into both. Getting to her feet proved to be more of a challenge—her legs shook with the effort of supporting herself. As she took tentative steps with her hands out to help her catch herself, it felt like her blood was starting to flow where it hadn't been for a long time.

By the time Kelly returned to peer around the door, she was solid on her feet and stretching her hands up. The girl said nothing, just opened the door to admit an older man, perhaps her father's age, though he seemed to have plenty of gray hairs among the light brown. He was clean shaven, his face long with soft edges and lines. His eyes were a middling shade, they could be nearly any color. As he saw her standing there, he smiled in an open, friendly, sympathetic way, which made him seem pleasant and trustworthy. Naturally, Chavali instantly disliked him because of it.

"I am Administrator Eldrack. It's nice to finally meet you,

Chavali." He offered his hand to shake with her. She stared at it, not sure she wanted to know anything in this man's thoughts. Not yet, anyway. Not until she had some idea of what was going on. When she didn't take it or respond within a few seconds, he pulled his hand back and clasped it together with his other, arms loose. "You do understand Shappan?"

"Yes." Something about his name tugged at a memory. She knew his name, somehow, from someplace. Kelly said it before, but only now did it seem familiar for some reason. "What is this place?"

Eldrack gestured to the door. "Let's take a walk."

She started to move slowly, figuring he was at least right that she needed to push herself a little. With each step, memories came loose. While she could recall her death in sharp detail, and her childhood was as clear as it was before, everything else was somewhat distant. Conversations, encounters, they came back into focus and she remembered. "Teryk, Eliot, and Colby, they work for you."

"What gives you that impression?" Letting her set the pace, he walked along beside her.

"Your name. I remember it." Indeed, he had a memorable name, a garble of sounds she wouldn't ever put together on purpose. "Teryk said he —" Wait, no he didn't. He only thought that, it never came out of his mouth.

Eldrack chuckled when she didn't finish the statement. "I see. It sounds like I'll have to speak with him the next time I see him. Yes, they work for me, in a manner of speaking. But that's jumping ahead. What do you remember?"

Chavali shivered. "I remember enough, but I do not understand."

He made a little 'hm' noise and nodded. "You died, Chavali. As near as could be told, it was by your own hand. I am indirectly responsible for you being here now, today. Neither I, this order, nor the kingdom of Shappa had anything to do with the attack on your clan, and all were unable to prevent or stop it. My agent discovered your body and brought it back here, where we have brought you back to life. A price was paid to do this, and for a reason."

It was somewhat comforting to know she did not dream any of that, to know it was real. Terrible, but real. "And such a cost, I imagine, must be repaid."

"Indeed. But you may choose. We can undo this, send you back to your grave, or you can live and repay the debt."

A fool's choice, really—no one in their right mind would choose to go back to death when she didn't have to. "I am unwilling to face death again, but I must ask how I will be erasing this debt."

"Of course. The goal of this order is to bring about the Reunion, and we work to that end, as would you. We are sponsored by Shappa, and owe that country fealty, as would you."

Reunion. The 'simple' task of tearing down the Creator's Divide and bringing Her back into the world. A fool's errand to go with a fool's choice. She smirked. "I see." Stopping, she turned to him. "I killed myself to stop a man from taking what he wanted. If presented with the same choice, I much doubt I would choose differently."

Eldrack regarded her seriously. "He was probably after your gift of prophecy? You saw your death as the only way to deny it to him?"

Taken aback by two such precise questions, Chavali blinked at him stupidly. "Yes."

He raised a hand to indicate a pledge. "No one in this order will harm you or force you to act without your consent. Should anyone ever do such a thing, report them to me, and I will see them punished for it accordingly. Does this address your concern satisfactorily?"

"Ah, yes." Chavali started walking again, still letting him lead her. "How long has this Order been around?"

"Quite a while. More details will have to wait, I'm afraid." Eldrack pushed open a door into a different room, this one blank and empty save for five women in loose brown and green robes with hoods to obscure their faces, standing around chatting. "Ladies," he said as a greeting. The women stopped talking immediately and moved to form a small circle in the center of the room. "Chavali, I must ask you to take a vow of obedience to this order before I can explain anything else. It's a simple thing, a protection for you as much as for us, but one with serious consequences for breaking. And, it is necessary. If you will not swear it, then you will go back to your death."

Chavali pursed her lips in mild annoyance, but nodded. If this was part of the price she must pay, then so be it. Eldrack already gave his own vow to her, it dispelled any true objections she had to all of this. It wasn't as if she had plenty of options. No, there was only one. "I accept this requirement."

His smile returned—it was strained, but fully genuine and spoke of satisfaction. "Into the middle of the circle, please." She complied, closed her eyes and just breathed while the women began to chant something she didn't understand. "Repeat after me," he said, his voice calm and full of strength. "I renounce my former life with all its trappings of individuals and wealth—lovers and enemies, plenty and poverty, friends and foes—I renounce them all." While she said these things back to him, his finger touched the back of her neck, lightly, barely. It wasn't his thoughts she sensed from him, but something else, something too great and wondrous to give her anything but awe.

"I give myself to the Fallen and their pursuit of the Greatest Sin and the hope of Reunion. I will repay the Creator and Shappa for my rebirth with five years of faithful service and may I be struck down with the Wasting should I violate the terms of our agreement." These were not mere words. Through the connection to Eldrack, which wasn't really to him, she felt the other presence reach inside her.

Power swelled in the room. That Something Other poured it down into her, through her, to the women and to Eldrack. The women chanted louder, the power flooded into her until she thought she would burst. She was filled with a sense of purpose, though she didn't yet know what that purpose was. The chanting hit a crescendo and Chavali exploded. Or so it felt. Everything died down and she collapsed, feeling dizzy and raw, but someone caught her.

Arms held her up, several of them, helped her get to the ground slowly so she could sit without hurting herself. Eldrack crouched beside her, a steadying hand on her shoulder. "It'll pass. Just breathe. Give it a minute."

Chavali nodded, but that made her more dizzy, so she stopped immediately and leaned forward to put her head in her hands. "Is it always like this?"

"I've never seen anyone fall over from it before, but it seemed normal to me otherwise." His voice held concern for her. "This is for you." He offered a ring, one just like those the three men wore when they visited the clan. "Around here, wear it on a finger, but outside, a necklace is just as good. However you choose to wear it, keep it on you at all times."

She slipped it onto her right ring finger, where it fit perfectly. Somehow, she felt clearer for having done so, the light-headedness fading already. Looking up, she met his eyes and asked the question she didn't want to know the answer to. "What of my clan?"

The answer was obvious before he opened his mouth. He pulled his hand away and sat on the floor while he sighed heavily. "I'm sorry. No one was left alive when we found your body. Most of the clan's possessions were destroyed, as well. We salvaged what we could, what was reasonable for you, but it isn't much. Nearly everything was burned."

It didn't feel real. She sat and stared blankly at Eldrack, unable to comprehend and internalize. "Where will I be staying?"

He nodded, still looking horribly sympathetic. Holding out his hand, he said, "I'll show you to your room."

Her stare shifted to his hand. This time, though, she said something. "I have uncontrolled telepathy, it happens through skin contact."

Eldrack blinked, then grew thoughtful. Whatever that revelation meant to him, though, he didn't explain. Instead, he grasped her arm where the sleeve covered it, allowing her to do the same with him, and helped her up like that. "Welcome to the Fallen. You're among family here." He let go as soon as she was on her feet and smiled kindly. "We have to go up stairs. A lot of stairs."

Chapter 9

The stairs were neverending. At ten flights up, she stopped counting. Finally, Eldrack steered her through an open doorway, though the wide spiral steps kept going upwards from there. They passed people on the stairs, a few of them in some kind of light colored uniform, most not. The ones not in uniforms were a highly varied lot. Some sported weapons, others didn't. Some dressed in plain, ordinary clothes, others in more flamboyant or elaborate costumes. There was nothing she could say for certain that applied to any of them as far as appearance was concerned. Not even all of them were human, though the majority were. She saw elves and half-breeds, even a dwarf.

It was all too much to take in right now. Chavali just put one bare foot in front of the other on the cool stone floor. Eldrack guided her to a small bedroom and left her there with a sad smile, shut the door and probably could hear it when she finally cracked and broke into tears in the center of that new space. Everything she had, everyone she'd ever known and cared about, all of it was gone. That man, whoever he was, he could have let them go when she killed herself. Instead, he slaughtered them all.

Two hundred and thirty-one people were slain out of pique for the loss of his prize. Some of them were young children, three were babies. She knew all their names, every single one. A few stood out, of course. Pasha, full of life. Biholtz, pleasant and thoughtful. Her parents. All of them, just gone. She was all that remained, the only one left to tell the stories to no one. The clan failed, it was just a memory now.

And, of course, Keino. That loss was deep and ached. She wanted him to leave her alone, but not forever, not like this. Worse, she didn't truly want him to leave her alone. What she really wanted was for him to understand that she was not his possession. She wanted for him to love her, not covet her. Out of the entire clan, she was the only person who could truly tell the difference, and he couldn't give her what she needed because of it. But she loved him anyway. Great stupid ass.

She only had so many tears to give before she fell asleep on the floor. When she woke up, feeling empty, she found someone put a blanket over her and left a covered plate and cup on the floor beside her. Staring at what must be food, she felt nothing at all, just blank numbness. All she had to do was reach over and pull the cover off, but she didn't. Her stomach growled, but she didn't care. Her throat was dry, but she didn't care. Her hand was asleep, but she didn't care.

No one came, no one checked on her, no one knocked on her door. This was what being alone felt like: blank, empty, pointless, defeated. Mamá was right, which hurt to accept. She never thought she would ever be left alone, but it happened. She never thought it would be the worst thing imaginable, but it was. She never thought the clan could die, but it did. Papá was always a strong man, it was impossible to imagine him as anything other than standing between his family and danger. Blaukenev men were like that, all of them.

Eventually, she needed to either get up or make a mess of herself. It was a difficult choice. In the end, the prospect of lying in a pool of her own waste to await a second death struck her as terribly unpleasant, especially given the oath she just took. Five years of this new life, that was what she offered to Eldrack, to this place. To repay the price of bringing her back. And then...what? Five years was a long time, long enough for many things to change.

Shaking her hand out to get the blood flowing through it again, she stretched her neck to try to dispel the stiffness caused by sleeping on the floor. She got slowly to her feet, letting the blanket fall, wondering what color it was and who brought it. This seemed a large place with plenty of people, so she had no real way to guess. It likely wasn't Eldrack, but it could have been Healer Kelly. Contemplating that mystery wasn't going to solve it, though.

Each step leaden, she plodded to her door. She stopped there, ran her fingers over the wood. It felt all wrong, it was completely different from a wagon door. All of this was so alien. How was she supposed to sleep in a bed by herself? It wasn't going to creak like a wagon. She wasn't going to accidentally pull Pasha's dreams into her own. Even listening to Luken and Zuli's passionate lovemaking would be missed, despite how annoying it was. Tears formed even as she smiled at how she hated listening to them, and to her parents, if only because it was a reminder of what she couldn't bear to have. She would give a great deal to have all the petty irritations back so she could have the rest of it, too.

But, she had to leave the room and find whatever facilities they used here before the matter became truly urgent. Wiping her face, she did her best to school the pain off it and stepped out, still in those boring dark clothes, still barefoot. There were two directions to go—it was a plain hall-way with more doors like her own, glowing globes of magic on the walls at regular intervals lighting the way. When Eldrack brought her here, she wasn't paying attention, so she didn't even know which way was which. Not that knowing would help her much, since she didn't know what she was even looking for or where it might be found.

Given the choices of standing still or picking a direction and going, she started walking, her hand brushing the wall, looking all around to take in whatever details she could to find the room again. In a place like this, one would expect they'd have numbers or some other marks on the doors, but she saw nothing. The best she could do was leave the door open so she could find it again by the contents. If anyone else had a blanket and tray on the floor, she might have a problem, but that seemed a remote possibility.

A woman stepped out of one of the doors ahead of her. She was about Chavali's age, in pants and a shirt that fit her well and showed off her athletic figure, with soft leather boots that hugged her calves all the way up to her knees. Her straight hair—a light brown or dark blonde—was cut short, above her ears, and she had a round face with a turned up nose. She noticed Chavali immediately and smiled brightly at her.

"You must be Chavali. I'm Portia."

Chavali nodded and stared at Portia's offered hand, not wanting to take it. The other woman's cheer felt disgraceful, like a slap in her face. "I am looking for something I do not know the Shappan words for," she said quietly. The effort of explaining this was significant, she didn't want to deal with these things. "I drank much water?"

Portia pulled her hand back, her smile dimmed a little, but she listened. "Oh, you need the washroom. It's this way, I'll show you."

"Washroom," Chavali repeated, but that didn't sound like the right thing to her. "I do not need washing." Actually, that may or may not be true. She was dead, after all. Normally, she bathed every few days, aside from washing her hands and face to wake herself up in the morning. Who knew what might be on her skin at this point. At any rate, a bath wasn't what she was trying to ask for.

"No, that's...ah, that's not all you do there. We just call it that. It's polite." Though her clan didn't follow such rules, Chavali spent enough time in foreign minds to grasp the idea of what was 'polite' and 'impolite', so she understood. Portia gestured for Chavali to follow. Now that it seemed clear they were speaking about the same thing, she did. "There should be other clothes for you to wear in your room, you can change whenever you want."

"I have not yet looked." It wasn't very far, just a few more doors down.

Portia pushed the door open for her, tapped the wall next to the door. "If you can't read Shappan, this says 'women'. We have separate washrooms for men and women here."

Chavali paused and stared at the wall, it was just blank stone so far as she could see. "I do not see anything there."

"Really?" Portia looked again, glanced at Chavali, frowned. "The stone is stained, right here." She tapped her finger on the wall again.

"Ah." This made sense now. "I cannot see colors. It must be the same shade as the stone. There are marks to identify the rooms, then, I expect. In the same stain."

Portia blinked and smirked. "Yeah, okay. I guess, um...I guess no one's ever had that problem before. It's kind of a bright orange color on blue-gray stone. Anyway, this is it."

Fortunately, Chavali had images from Outsiders' minds to explain how to use the facilities she found within. Otherwise, what she found would have mystified her. Thank goodness those memories actually had some use, because they were repulsive to sit through at the time. Portia paced in and splashed some water on her face, waiting for Chavali to be finished.

"This can be kind of an intimidating, confusing place when you first get here, but it's not really all that bad once you get the hang of it," Portia said as Chavali paced back out to where she was. "I grew up on a pig farm, personally. This place is total luxury compared to that, they really spared no expense. Between magic and engineering, we've got just about everything we need here to turn into fat, pampered house cats."

She actually could use a bath right now. There were tubs off to one side, a partial wall separating the two spaces, and she went over there to have a look. Each one was big enough to lounge in. "How do I make these work?" Curiosity was getting the better of her, pushing the aching away, at least for the moment.

Portia smiled and walked over, showed her how to use the taps to get hot or cold water. That she was surprised to see Chavali strip down and climb right in showed on her face. "Uh, do you want some privacy?"

"I do not care." Hot water, at her command! Chavali sighed with the simple pleasure of sitting in a tub while it filled.

Getting over her reaction to Chavali quickly, Portia grinned. "I guess you're from someplace rural like me, then?"

"My clan travels in wagons, we bathe in half barrels or rivers. Our mage, Alazne, has a magic she does to make our mess small, to leave the places we stay in good condition." Chavali's face fell. "Traveled. They—" She choked a little, unable to say it out loud yet.

"I'm sorry." Portia sounded like she was sincerely sorry. "When I was killed, I lost some people I cared about, too. It happens to a lot of us."

Chavali turned off the water and sat there, soaking, watching the ripples in the surface. "It hurts."

"Yeah. But it won't always. It's been three years for me, and I still miss them, but it doesn't hurt like it used to, not anymore."

Dunking her head, Chavali stayed underwater for a short time, wondering if she could will herself to drown. That would be easier, it would hurt less. Everything would hurt less. She surfaced again, though, unable to force herself to open her mouth. Because she wanted to live, and denying it was stupid. Pain, she knew that well enough. There was nothing to compare to the agony of a prophecy, nothing at all. This was not worse than that, not even close. She could still think, she could still move, she could still be. This would not be so easily soothed, but she was a coward if she couldn't face it.

"They are all dead." How flat and distant her voice sounded bothered her. "All of them. My whole clan is nothing now."

Portia looked away, grew pensive. "All of them, but not you."

"Apparently, someone has to go on so tears can be shed. Without me, no one would mourn them." Such bitterness, did she really think that, feel that?

Shaking her head, Portia gave her a sad smile. "I mean that techni-cally, your clan isn't dead, because you're still alive. You can carry it on. Bring in new people and start over. It won't bring back the people you cared about, but it will bring back the clan."

There were reasons that wasn't true, could never be true, but Chavali wasn't going to discuss them. Not here, not now, not with a total stranger. Portia was nice, and Chavali already understood these Fallen were a family of sorts, but it wasn't the same, and couldn't ever be the same. Lying back, she let her hair soak in the water, breathed deeply. "Perhaps. Someday."

Portia went quiet and let Chavali soak in peace for a few minutes. "Would you like me to leave? You seem like you want to be alone."

Chavali couldn't help it, she started to laugh. It quickly became hysterical, then segued into tears. She covered her face and sat up, didn't notice the water draining out of the tub until Portia put a towel over her shoulders, then helped her stand up and wrapped her in another one. She guided Chavali back to her room, by which time the tears were actually winding down. It took that long to put one foot in front of the other.

"There should be clothes in the drawers, and that basket," Portia pointed to the large one sitting in the corner next to the bed, "should have anything they found with you that wasn't destroyed. The clothes are plain and boring, but they're clothes. You can get new stuff later. Do you need any help?"

"No, I think I will be fine now, thank you." Chavali stood there in the middle of her room in two towels, wondering how she would ever force herself to accept staying in one place. Admittedly, the luxury of the bathtubs would be helpful, but it was still disturbing and foreign. "You should go do whatever you were going to do when I interrupted you."

"Okay. Don't be afraid to wander around. If there's someplace you're not supposed to be, you won't be able to get there without someone telling you not to. Just knock if a door is closed and you can't tell what it is."

Chavali nodded her understanding and summoned up a pathetically weak smile for Portia as the other woman left the room, shutting the door carefully behind herself. There was the matter of her stomach, which she chose to deal with first. The food was, mercifully, all things that didn't need to be kept warm or cold to taste good. She picked at it without bothering to poke around the room, just trying to not think very much.

When she did eventually get up to look through the drawers, she found just what Portia said: plain clothes. She picked out a shirt with long sleeves and put a sleeveless dress over that, as that was the bulk of the options. There were also pants, but she was more comfortable in a dress. The socks and shoes were unremarkable, meant to be worn indoors, where it was neither hot nor cold and had a floor.

Once clothed, she pulled the beads and wet feather out of her hair. She should have taken them out before the bath. It would be a while before they were dry. Using a wooden comb she found in one of the drawers, she found herself staring at the basket in the corner. Curiosity warred with dread; anything inside would just remind her of those she lost, and even considering opening that basket filled her mind with images of the people she lost.

Looking away from it, she determinedly did not cry as she finished combing her hair out. Then she left the room, putting some distance between herself and the basket. Again, she left the door open, this time just a little. Later, she would find a way to deal with this problem. For now, she wandered, her fingers brushing the wall. There was the washroom, the door was spaced differently from the others. A second oddly spaced door was probably the men's washroom. She did not make an effort to find out.

At the end of the hall, which had branches and seemed to go on a rather long way, she found a room with no door in the doorway. No one was inside it. The floor was covered with thick rugs, it had well cushioned armchairs scattered around with tables, interesting tapestries hung on some of the walls, bookshelves with books and scrolls on other walls, and a single bank of cabinets. Interesting that she hadn't seen any windows yet.

With no one around to explain anything, she didn't bother going inside, just continued her tour. There was also a large empty room with the door standing open, she wasn't sure what it was for. Several stands lined one wall, pieces of thick wood with planks for feet to keep them upright, which confused her. This wasn't a good time to be confused like that, so she moved on. There were, she thought, thirty doors that were probably rooms like her own, all arrayed in one direction from the spiral stair. When she found herself back at that, she looked up, then down. Voices echoed in the chamber, but they could be anywhere, and she elected to go down. That was where she came from with Eldrack.

Half a turn down the stairs, she discovered another doorway and went through it. Very quickly, she determined it was exactly like the one above, but this one had voices coming from it. Going towards them, she found herself at this floor's empty room, except it wasn't empty. Two men fought each other with blades, she recognized it as sparring from having watched the activity often enough. The other thing she recognized was one of the men—Colby, that very tall soldier who visited her clan.

Her eyes slid right over the other man to focus on Colby, who had no shirt on and was using his large sword expertly. This explained why the room was so large and had such a high ceiling: it had to accommodate men like this, fighting like that. Leaning against the doorway with her arms crossed, she watched in silence. He had a handful of scars scattered across him—some looked like burns, the rest were more likely from weapons. He was well muscled and in good shape.

Not long after she took up that post, he noticed her standing there, frowned, and took a solid whack to the side for it. The other man had enough sense to twist his own blade to hit him with the flat, or Colby might have been seriously injured. He grunted with pain and his attention was immediately back on his opponent.

"Sorry, man, are you okay?" The other man was probably a foot shorter than Colby, making him still at least a half foot taller than Chavali. He reached out to offer Colby a hand to steady himself.

Waving off the help, Colby checked where he was hit, finding a thin line of blood, but the cut was superficial. "Yeah, fine." He pointed at Chavali. "I need to work on ignoring distractions, I guess."

The other man looked over and chuckled. After wiping his blade off on his pants, he sheathed it. "It was probably time to stop anyway. See you later."

"Yeah, probably." Colby went to where his shirt lay on the floor and used it to daub hesitantly at the blood.

The other man nodded to Chavali in greeting as he dodged around her to get through the doorway. She returned the nod, but watched Colby. "It seems you remember me."

Colby looked up and his expression was cautious. "I do."

How easily she fell back into being suspicious of him and his motives, even now that she had a much better idea of what they were, even when she had so many other things pressing on her. "I did not intend to distract you enough to be hurt. I am sorry for that."

Peeling the shirt away, he checked the wound, then pressed the shirt back again. "It's okay. It was my fault I got hit." He hefted the sword over his shoulder and made to leave the room. "When did you wake up?"

"Yesterday, I think. I have not yet seen the sun, so I am not sure." Since he didn't seem to mind her company, she turned and walked with him to wherever he was going. His stride was ground devouring, but he slowed it so she could keep up.

"It's easy to lose track of time down here, yeah."

"Down?"

Colby nodded—he was uncomfortable, though she wasn't sure why. To be fair, this was an odd situation, and she was uncomfortable, too. Something about having been adversaries just a week or so ago and now allies. "We're underground."

That certainly explained the lack of windows. Chavali looked up for no reason, only seeing the stone ceiling. "It is allowed to go up and out?"

"Sure. Just keep going up until you can't anymore. They'll let you back in because of the ring." He stopped in front of a door and gestured towards it. "This is my room."

"Ah." She was never going to be able to find it again. That was fine, except it felt like there was something unfinished here. But, he was opening his door and going in, and she was just standing there, not saying anything. It was a queer feeling, being the one who wasn't sure what to say or do. She wasn't even sure why she had no idea what to do. Probably, it was because she was too busy keeping her grip on herself to pay attention to anything else.

Before closing the door, he looked at her, surprised she was still standing there. "I really need to at least change my clothes. Was there something you wanted from me?"

Blinking stupidly, Chavali shook her head. "No. Nothing." She turned awkwardly and walked away. Thankfully, he shut the door before she realized she was going the wrong way to reach the stairs. Her initial impulse as she started up the steps again was to go back to her room and hide there until someone came to check if she was still alive, that she might have more time to get her head back on straight. But that was no less cowardly than drowning herself. Instead, she kept going up and up. This time, she was counting the floors, because that was only way she would ever find her room again.

Seven floors up, the stairs ended at a heavy stone door. For a moment, she worried about how she would manage to heave that thing anywhere, but someone coming in opened it from the other side. She heard a clank and something sliding, then it swung towards her. The person opening it, she didn't recognize—he was a thin man with tired eyes, about her own height, probably younger than her, wearing a wool cloak lined with fur over heavy clothes and boots. He held the door open for her, but looked to be in a hurry, so she didn't do more than return the simple nod of greeting he gave her. On this side, it was a hallway with no doors, one that didn't go very far before it turned.

Closing the door behind her was thankfully taken care of by that thin man, but this meant she wasn't completely certain how to get back down. A problem for later. Right now, she forged onward, moving through a twisting, turning corridor that had no apparent purpose in its length other than to take a long time to get from one end to the other. When she finally found the stairs at the other end, they were wide and straight, each step longer than it needed to be, though they were of a rather normal height.

The steps went up more than a full flight, then opened into a vast chamber, one that must be large enough to fit all the clan's wagons, four or five times over. It was empty of anything but three people standing in roughly the middle, chatting, their voices echoing to her without being intelligible. It was two women and one man, all three engaged in what seemed a conversation of interest. As she got closer, she could tell they spoke a language she didn't understand, and so passed them by without interrupting.

Whoever designed this place certainly had a love affair with stairs. The next set of them was narrow and tightly spiraled up to a dead end, but there was a lever. After hesitating for a moment, she pulled it down. The wall in front of her—wood instead of stone—swung open, away from her.

It put her in yet another stone room, and this one was far from empty. It was a cellar full of boxes and barrels that smelled like beer. And more stairs. A flight of steps on the other side of the room made her sigh lightly. She wove around the boxes and shelves to reach and climb it. The door this time was plain wood, and on the other side, she was greeted by the sound of voices and someone playing a stringed instrument of some kind.

She emerged into...a tavern. From Outsider memories, she knew that word applied and stood there, dumbfounded by the sight. All of that climbing and walking was to reach a tavern. It had windows, though, and she walked over to one to see outside. Thick gray clouds covered the sky and fat flakes of snow fell onto what looked like the center of a small town with a fountain in the middle. Everything was covered already with a few inches of the stuff.

The day she died, it was late summer and the trees were probably a few weeks from starting to turn. Either she was on some island far north of the continent, or she was dead longer than she thought. Eldrack mentioned Shappa, so she assumed she was in that country. How long ago was her clan slaughtered? How long did her body lie there before they came and found it, ravaged by flies and animals and weather? She lifted her hand, the one with the ring on it, and looked it over, wondering how much had to be repaired, how long that took.

"Can I get you anything?" The young woman who spoke was pleasant and fresh-faced, her nose and cheeks covered with a mass of freckles. She wore a plain dress with an apron over it and had her hair up in a bonnet.

Chavali opened her mouth, but shut it again, not sure what to say or do. Again. "I have nothing to pay with," she finally answered when the girl's friendly smile faltered a little bit.

The girl leaned in and spoke more softly. "Are you new here?"

It was something of a relief that the girl guessed so easily, though it should have been a major annoyance. "Yes."

"Thought so." She pointed to the ring without being forceful or obvious about it. "We have tea, coffee, and a light ale you can have for free because of that."

"Ah. Tea, please." Chavali slipped into a chair by the window, wanting to watch the snow fall for a while. If she was dressed for it, she would go outside, but this was close enough. A minute or so later, the girl brought her a cup of steaming tea, then she was left alone, staring outside and sipping at the mug. The front door opened several times as she sat, people coming and going, but she paid it no attention.

Perhaps a half hour passed before a voice startled her out of her vague staring. "I'm truly sorry to be meeting again this way." Teryk stood there, snow on his cloak and in his pale beard just starting to melt. "May I sit?"

"Yes." She pushed her cup away, it was empty. The facial hair didn't really suit him, he looked better clean-shaven, but it was winter. Many of the men of the clan let theirs grow out to stave off the cold, too. The dead men of the dead clan.

The girl came by, he waved her off. "How long since you woke up?"

"A day, perhaps, I am not sure. Can I ask you how long since we met before?"

Teryk pulled off a heavy glove and scratched at his beard. "Ah, that would be...three, maybe four months now."

Turning back to the window, she sighed lightly. "That is a long time to be a corpse."

"You were probably raised not long after you died, it just takes some of us a long time to recover from the process." He paused for a few moments, looked away then back. "You said the feather was a sort of rank thing. Was that true?"

"Yes." She felt no compulsion to speak the complete truth here, and still had secrets to keep, even if they were only for herself. "It is grown into the bone. My position was for life. When I died, they were supposed to smash my skull and crack the feather out to pass it on to the next Seer."

"Oh. Huh." Teryk made some noise, Chavali turned enough to see him pulling his cloak off and setting it on the empty chair beside himself. "Do you need to talk about it?"

"No." That wasn't entirely true. "Maybe. I do not know."

"Do you want to borrow my cloak to go outside?"

Her eyes were drawn to the cloak and she found herself nodding. "Yes, please."

He passed it over with a small smile. "I'll wait here."

"Thank you." Standing up, she threw the cloak over her shoulders and pulled it close, then hurried out the door. It was, as expected, freezing, and the snow fell faster than it looked from inside. The banks on the sides of the road were about a foot high already, with a few inches in the road-way. Her shoes weren't really meant for this, but she didn't care. They could dry out when she got back to her room.

She moved enough to be out of the way of anyone who might want to go past her, then turned up her face to the sky, blinking rapidly at flakes falling into her eyes. This was real. Her clan was dead. She was alive. There was something for her to do here. That something was stupid, she didn't really believe Reunion was truly possible, and couldn't explain why she never felt it would actually be a terribly good thing regardless, but it was a purpose, the one that entity wanted her to pursue.

Her soul was pledged to that task. Knowing that, feeling that, there was no other option but to accept all of this and get busy doing it. Her clan was dead, it would never live again, not if the only way was by her bearing children, but she was still here and could carry it on until she died. While one Blaukenev yet lived, all would.

Chapter 10

Chavali draped the cloak back over the chair next to Teryk and found her mug full of hot tea again. He now had a mug of something, also, and sat patiently at the table. He smiled at her and it was pleasant, friendly, sympathetic. Was everyone here like that? She supposed they were all bound together by that pledge, the least they could do was make a token effort at getting along. It was even possible he felt guilty somehow for her being here.

She put her hands around her mug after she sat down again and sipped at it, the warmth welcome after the frigid air outside. Her shoes and socks were soaked, but she'd live for a little while. "How long will the winter last?"

"Another three months or so." Teryk watched her. It looked like he was trying to puzzle her out somehow. He took a long drink from his mug and sighed. "It's nice here in the spring. They have a party as soon as it's warm enough, there's music and dancing. The food isn't spectacular, because nothing's growing yet by then, but it's a lot of fun anyway."

Chavali nodded and sipped at her tea. "We celebrate life often. Everyone's birthday is special, even the ones that happen all at the same time." She stopped herself before she said anything about Estevior's Feast, leaving a pause she knew was awkward without being able to decide what to fill it with.

"There were two hundred-some people, weren't there? The whole clan celebrated every single birthday?"

"Yes. The whole clan is one unit, one thing. To be fair, though, many of the birthdays fall in the same..." She trailed off as she noticed she was using present tense again, speaking about them as if they were alive still. Shutting her eyes, she sighed heavily. "Fell. The birthdays fell in the same span of a month or so." At least she wasn't collapsing into tears out here.

Teryk still sounded sympathetic, damn him. "I remember what you said about clan, about how it runs deep. I'm amazed you're not a basket case."

Opening her eyes again, she looked down at her mug, at her hands. A thumb idly rubbed the rim. "I am the Seer." That was a full explanation, as far as she was concerned.

Since she wasn't looking at him, she didn't really see his reaction, but when he set his cup back down, it seemed like the act rang with a note of finality. He stood up, slid his chair back under the table. "I'm going in," he said, as if he felt a need to explain.

Right now, Chavali wished she could just run to her family's wagon and hide inside. Looking up at him, she saw he watched her still. "Do you mind if I walk with you? I do not understand the doors so well."

He nodded, picked up his cloak as she stood, and gestured for her to come with him. "The first two floors are set up the way they are for defensive purposes. In the event the Tower here is ever attacked, they're rigged to turn into trap-filled nightmares." In the cellar, he showed her how to open and shut the door properly from each side.

Knowing how to get in and out was more interesting than any possible questions she might have, so she held them until they were at the bottom of this first set of stairs. The vast chamber was empty now. "What about the village?"

"They have defenses, and most of the people who live here are trained in various forms of combat. Some of them are retired mercenaries and soldiers, others are Healers who no longer serve below for one reason or another. In an attack, if they can't get to their own refuges, they can come down here. Also, the bartender in the tavern is a lot more than he looks like."

Chavali lifted an eyebrow at that particular wording. "Is he a dragon, then?" she offered in jest, though her ability to express humor was stunted right now.

Teryk took her question seriously and shrugged. "Ask him if you want to know about him. All I'll say is he's not defenseless."

The statement made Chavali turn back and look even though there was nothing to see. "This is a major operation."

"Yes. Yes, it is. We have the backing of the King of Shappa, and he supports our goal here."

Uninterested in discussing that particular goal, Chavali pushed it away and left a pause in the conversation to avoid startling him with an unexpected change of subject. "Is it a rude thing to ask here, about how people died, and how long ago?"

"Rude?" Teryk rubbed his chin thoughtfully. "No, not as a matter of course. Some people won't want to talk about it, but I don't think anyone would consider it rude. Especially not from a new person. I wouldn't open with that or anything, but you shouldn't be afraid to ask."

"May I ask about yours, then?" She didn't care and wasn't sure why she asked, except that she was so used to being surrounded by people she knew absolutely everything about. Point to anyone in the clan and she could tell quite a bit about them, all their most embarrassing and proudest moments, even for the Elders. Here, she knew nothing about anyone, beyond a handful of names.

He didn't answer immediately and she could tell he wasn't excited about the subject as they started down the stairs to the long, twisting hallway level. At the bottom, he sighed. "I guess I did set myself up for that. Someone tried to kill my father, and I got in the way."

Everything he said back at the clan camp was still rather fresh for her, and she remembered all her impressions of him just fine. "He is some sort of Mecalle nobility, yes?"

Stunned by the question, he stopped and looked at her. "How could you possibly know that?"

"I am a Seer." Normally, she said this and people left it be, taking her to be what she said she was. This time, the statement felt a little flat, like she was trying to convince herself as much as him. Really, how could she rightfully call herself that when she hadn't seen the attack on her clan coming? Why didn't the spirits tell her it was going to happen? They were supposed to help her protect the clan.

He grabbed her arm where it was covered by her sleeve, not accepting the answer. "No, really. How did you know that?"

Like this, she was actually afraid of him. It wasn't that she thought he could—or would—hurt her, it was more that she didn't know what he would tell others, how he might poison the well, so to speak, making it difficult for her to navigate the social waters here. With clan, she tried not to lie much, keeping the air clear. This was like clan, in a way, and she needed to accept that, to believe it. There were many things she couldn't—or wouldn't—tell them, but the truth about simple matters wasn't among them. "I could tell when you visited the clan. It sits on you like a mantle, and your accent is plain enough. Half of fortune telling is reading people, by their words and behavior."

Frowning, he let go of her, retracting his hand like it did something wrong and he knew it. "Oh. Right." He turned awkwardly and started walking again. "I've been here for four years, I'm really used to the idea of no one knowing who I am, and that being important. It's a little...suspicious, I guess, when someone does."

"Rest assured," she said, not wanting to upset him further, "I have no idea who your father actually is."

He nodded and said nothing else, leading her through the rest of the long hallway. At the end, he showed her how to use that door. The urge to ask another question was strong, but she wanted to avoid irritating him too much. Still, when he started down the main stairs at a brisk pace she had no hope of keeping up with, she said something before he got too far to hear it. "Did he live?"

"What?" He stopped and looked back up at her, confused by the question.

"Your father, did he live through the attack?"

Teryk grunted and started back down. "No. My sister has the title now."

That was probably the very short version of a gripping story, but he was in no mood to relate it now. Another time, perhaps, she would get him to tell her the tale. Following at a much slower pace, she looked at the next doorway she came to, trying to decide what to do with herself. If she went back to her room, she would have to stare at that awful basket and have nothing else to distract herself with.

She remembered Portia saying that she could go anywhere she wasn't told she couldn't, and decided to investigate what lay beyond this doorway. On her way up, she only just barely glanced through each of these, but now went through to see what there was to be seen. It was a small area with four other doors. An older man in white shirt and pants sat in a cushioned wood chair, doing something with tools to a shirt of chain-mail, possibly repairing it.

As soon as she walked in, he looked up and smiled pleasantly at her, his weathered face crinkling up with it. His hands still held the armor and his tools, ready to take up the task again if she needed no help from him. "Don't believe we've met, Miss. Can I help you with anything?"

"I am new," she confirmed. "What is it that you could help me with?"

He snorted and rolled his eyes. "I really wish Eldrack would set up an orientation for you new people. No, he says, everyone is ready in their own time, and we shouldn't press anyone to take in new information before they're ready. Bah. Bah, I say! You're alive, get on with living already."

Taken aback by the tirade, Chavali stood there, blinking at him. "I can come back later," she offered. "Though it seems you offer nothing I might need here."

The man chuckled and set the armor aside. "No, no, don't go. I'm Kiron, I take care of armor and weapons here. We keep a lot of spares lying around in case the Tower ever needs defending, and when weapons get broken, I fix or replace them. Got a smithy in the back and everything, but I don't need it to fix chain."

"Ah. I do not use weapons or armor, but perhaps you could instead give me information."

She was going to say more, but he interrupted her, looking her over skeptically. "Don't use weapons at all? Even the ponciest mages use a staff or a short blade of some kind."

"I do not know this word 'ponciest'." She frowned at him, because she didn't think much of the attitude he showed her. People didn't behave like this towards the clan Seer. "But it does not matter. No, I have no training with weapons. What I actually need is clothing, winter things."

He sighed heavily and shook his head like he thought she was making a terrible mistake. "Someone down here could teach you to defend yourself. The basics aren't hard to pick up, just takes practice. When you decide to be sensible, you come back and visit me, Kiron. I'll set you up with a nice weapon, whatever kind you want. Until then, what you want is on the next floor down. The one below that has things you might want for your room."

His manner annoyed her, but she gave him a polite nod and backed out as he returned to his task. "Thank you." The next floor down had the same entry point, a small room with four doors, but instead of an annoying old man, there were three young women in white. One, the brunette, was in pants and a shirt, the other two were both blonde and wore dresses. The blondes looked entirely too similar to be anything other than twins. They sat in chairs, chatting amiably, and looked at her with cheerful smiles as she entered.

"Hi," the brunette said, far too chipper for Chavali's mood. "I'll bet you're looking for clothes." She stood up and beckoned her forward, the other two also stood. "Do those fit alright, or would you like some- thing tighter?"

"These are fine. I only came for winter things, to go outside." All three of them looked at her like that was a silly thing to say.

"Oh," the brunette said, like she wasn't sure if she was about to offend Chavali and actually cared about that. "It's just, those aren't really very flattering colors for you."

Both of the blondes nodded, one said, "You'd look much nicer in something with a pinkish tint, which you must know since it's all in your hair."

Chavali sighed and stifled back annoyance and frustration and aching. Pasha liked to do this kind of thing, to choose her clothes and help her dress. "I do not especially care. A cloak and boots, mittens and a scarf, heavy socks. These are the things I came for."

All three women looked quite put out, which annoyed Chavali even more. "Are you sure?" The brunette seemed so convinced no one could possibly mean what she said and be serious.

"Forget it." Chavali turned around and walked right back out of the room, unwilling to deal with them. In a few days, perhaps, that sort of thing wouldn't bother her, but it was more than she could take right now. They thought they were cute, amusing, lighthearted. Perhaps they were, just not to her. She ignored the voice that asked her to come back, hurrying down to her own floor. The rest of this wretched place could wait.

At least no one stopped her from retreating to her room, where she stared at the wall for a long time. Here she was, given a second chance at life, and it was such a foreign place, it was like being actually reborn. If only she could shut off the ache of loss, she might be curious about everything, looking for new stories and experiences. Instead, all she wanted to do was sit and stare at the wall until everything unfamiliar and painful went away.

A soft knock on her door pulled her out of the blankness she settled into, a kind of staticky feeling of nothing. For several seconds, she turned her empty stare on the door, almost confused by it as her mind struggled to wake up again. "Come in," she called, her voice harsh for not being used for a while.

The door opened slowly, Portia stood there. "Hey," she said with a muted, tentative smile. "Would you like to come down for a meal with me? It's about dinnertime, and I figured you might not know where to go."

Chavali blinked a few times and stared at Portia. Vaguely, she was aware of being a little hungry, so she nodded and slid off her bed. "No, I do not know where it is."

Her smile faltering a little, Portia took Chavali's arm and started walking with her. "The dining hall is on level nineteen."

"What level is this one?" Chavali didn't squirm against the contact, and Portia didn't take her hand, just looped their arms together in a friendly sort of way.

"Ten. So, we get to go down nine floors to eat. On the bright side," she said with a grin, "having to go so far means you can indulge a little when you want to without worrying about it going straight to your hips."

"I am not especially worried about my hips." For clan, Chavali was a little meaty, mostly because she spent so much time sitting. It never once crossed her mind to be concerned or to worry about such things. No one cared what she looked like. If she grew too large for her costume, it would be altered to fit her better.

Portia shrugged. "My mother always used to tell me that I should just strap sweets to my thighs instead of eating them, it's the same outcome."

Chavali had no idea how to respond to that. No one worried about such things in the clan. What difference did it make if a woman's thighs were a bit large? So long as she could do everything she needed to, it was fine. Men of the clan wouldn't turn down a woman for sex just because she was bigger than others. Outsider men weren't much different—at least, not the ones whose minds she'd been in.

"Ah," she finally said, because Portia seemed like she expected an answer of some kind. The rest of the trip down the stairs was made in relative silence. Portia waved to a few people they passed, but didn't start any conversations with them. She pointed out the library, which was spread across two floors—one was for general knowledge, the other for reports and treatises on subjects pertinent to the pursuit of Reunion. There were meeting rooms and larger, better equipped practice rooms than the ones on the living quarters floors, and plenty of places with writing tools and such things. Chavali wasn't terribly interested in any of it. She just filed away the information in case she needed it later.

The nineteenth floor had a grand room full of round tables with six chairs each. It could probably seat two hundred at once, which was far more than it needed right now. Twenty-seven people, sixteen of them women, currently sat scattered across those tables, none by themselves. The light chatter was too little to fill the whole hall or be constant, and the place felt so empty. Nothing with the clan ever felt this empty, not even Chavali's work tent.

At one end, it was set up as a buffet. Portia let go of her to grab two plates. "So, everything here is self-service. The staff—that's everyone in the white uniforms—keeps the food edible and takes care of the whole she-bang. Dirty plates go over there," she pointed to a bin. "If you ever want something specific, you can request it, but there's a lot of people here, so try to avoid it. Also, if you want to make something yourself, you're free to, just try to do it at off-peak times."

"I am not much of a cook, there is no worry for me doing this." The long tables had more than enough different things to try to keep her from caring much anyway. The bread section alone had ten different varieties, most of which were new to her. Her clan didn't make many kinds of bread; they didn't have ovens, just fires.

"Me neither, but there are some people who really get into it. There's a guy, Colby, he makes the best blueberry pancakes I've ever had."

Chavali recalled how he wanted to know about herbs and such things, found herself nodding. "Something to keep in mind."

When they reached a table near but not next to the other occupied ones, Portia pointed people out. "Agatha, she's a priest and lives on our floor, has a mean backhand swing with her mace. That's Violet sitting with her, also on our floor. She's an acrobat and contortionist." Portia seemed to know at least a little about everyone present, ticking off the names and specialties as if reading from a list. The recitation of ability was a little staggering. From spellcasters to trapsmiths to swordfighters, it seemed everyone had something to make herself useful in at least a few unpleasant situations.

It was daunting, and humbling. What could Chavali do? If she was lucky, talk someone out of trying to kill her, perhaps distract them by telling stories. This wasn't a comforting thought. She focused on her food and tried not to dwell on the subject much. Kiron suggested she should learn, maybe he was right. It was just counter to how she was raised. The Seer didn't need to defend herself, that's why she had a bodyguard. And one more thing to deal with, not to mention she wasn't sure who to ask for such lessoning. Probably, Kiron could offer suggestions, but taking this kind of instruction from a stranger felt wrong.

"That's a pretty serious frown." Portia let her brood until her own food was mostly gone, but Chavali's plate was barely touched. "Do you want to talk about it?"

Sighing heavily, Chavali shook her head, but finished with a shrug. "I am not certain what 'it' is."

Nodding knowingly, Portia smiled sympathetically. "Maybe you should go talk to your Healer, those women are devilish in their ability to draw out poison from wounds, mental and physical."

"What do you mean 'my' Healer?" It was an odd choice of words, even with her imperfect understanding of Shappan.

Portia shrugged and waved off the question. "The one who was there when you woke up. She's sort of in charge of your case, you might say."

That explanation didn't quite seem honest, and definitely wasn't satisfactory, but Chavali didn't want to press about it. "Ah. I suppose I could."

"You can find her by asking on the next level down. If she's not around, someone can fetch her for you." When Chavali started to get up, Portia put out a hand to stop her. "Eat first."

Her interest and appetite hadn't increased in the slightest, but she ate anyway, stuffing the food in and chewing mechanically. A half hour later, after parting with Portia, she sat in a small room, waiting. One of the white-clad staff went to find Healer Kelly for her, leaving her here. It was a nice room, as such things went. The two chairs were well cushioned, covered with something like velvet but not quite as plush in an ordinary beige color. The floor had a thick rug in a matching color, and there were two potted plants with large leaves in the far corners. It had no table or desk and looked like a place designed specifically to sit and talk privately.

The wait wasn't long. Healer Kelly opened the door about five minutes after Chavali was left here, looking about the same as before, but without the silly hat. Her straight, coppery hair was pulled back in a ponytail—it probably reached her shoulders when it was loose. A precisely cut line of bangs hung halfway down her forehead. "Hi, I hope you weren't sitting here too long." Her smile was pleasant and sympathetic, just like everyone else's. Without turning away from Chavali, she shut the door behind herself and sat in the other chair.

"No, not at all." It was a queer sensation, to be looking for serious help with something so personal and delicate in the first place. Asking an Outsider for this was difficult, even beyond difficult. Her instincts screamed at her to fish for information even though she was here because she needed someone to talk to and felt an odd connection to this woman, even to the point that she trusted Kelly for no reason to be discreet and not to mock her. "I am sorry for bothering you."

"It's no bother at all." The way she said it wasn't dismissing the concern so much as making clear it was unfounded. "This and providing healing are my entire job. Never feel like you're bothering me when you need to talk, just come down and do it."

"I see." The openness in the other woman's gaze, especially given she was at least a few years younger, bothered Chavali and made her look down at her hands, now clasped together in her lap. It wasn't that honesty unnerved her so much as that it came from someone she didn't know, whose motives she had no clue about. To all appearances, Kelly wanted to help her because she actually wanted to help her, which was bizarre.

Healer Kelly looked at her for several long, empty seconds, then said, "I've heard you're from a clan, and it was tightly knit. I guess the idea of coming to someone outside it for anything like this is probably foreign. That's okay. You don't really have to say anything if you don't want to. If all you really need me for is to have someone sit here with you, I can do that."

Chavali hated it when people did that to her. She did it to others all the time, but very few people managed to do it in return, and it was always unnerving. It was supposed to be something she could do that others couldn't, supposed to be something she had no peer in. Among the clan, this was fully true, and her clients were rarely adept at reading people or knowing what was going on underneath. Now, though, she was surrounded by people who could, and it was disturbing.

She only let a short time pass before she said, "I wish you spoke the language of my clan. These things are difficult at best in Shappan. I know it decently well, but sometimes, the words I do not know make everything much harder."

"I wish I did, too, then." Kelly meant this. "I'm actually from the village above, so Shappan is all I speak. Maybe you could teach me."

"No." Chavali shook her head without giving it even a single thought. "This is forbidden, an act of..." The proper word was 'treason', but how much did it really apply anymore? She was the clan now, and she could decide to do whatever she wanted, traditions and strictures be damned. Except that she wasn't sure of the consequences. Certainly, there was no harm in teaching it to an Outsider who married into the clan. Indeed, they needed to learn it to survive. Just someone to talk to, that might cause some kind of problem she couldn't foresee. "A wrong thing."

Ever so slightly taken aback by the immediate reaction, Healer Kelly blinked a few times. "You feel the rules of your clan still apply, even though you're the only one left?"

"Yes, of course." Chavali waved off the question, but still answered it. "I am the clan, it is me, I am it. These rules do not stop being relevant simply because I am the only one around to enforce them on myself. The ways of the clan have reasons behind them, even if we— Even if I have forgotten or never learned some of them. Clearly, some are no longer feasible. I cannot live in a wagon or be ever traveling anymore, for example. The ones I can follow, though, I will."

"It's hard to let go of the things that mattered most," Healer Kelly said. She thought she understood what was going on, that was clear, but this part wasn't about grief.

"No, no, that is not it." Chavali frowned and tried to think of a way to explain this that didn't say more than she ought to but did close the topic satisfactorily. "It is part of...part of me, part of what I am. You are a Healer, I am the clan Seer. This does not end until I am dead. When I take a husband, he will be clan then, and we will rebuild what was lost in what ways we can."

"You don't really want to take a husband, though."

Her face went sour, both at the assertion and the fact that Kelly noticed. "It is not my ideal choice, no. There is no one else, though. It must be through me anyone new comes into the clan. This is not a subject I wish to discuss. It is complex and difficult, not to be untangled by a well meaning Outsider who knows only the color of the cloth and nothing else." She may have been a little sharper than was necessary, but this was important.

"Sorry," Healer Kelly said, abashed and blushing. "I was given training for this, but I haven't really done it before. I just want to help. Whatever you want to talk about, we can talk about that."

The girl irritated Chavali on several levels, but if she was assigned to her, whatever that truly meant, she supposed she ought to at least give her Healer a real chance. "Perhaps it would be better if we speak of less weighty things for now." She turned the subject to the less perilous one of general Tower etiquette, going beyond the simple inquiry she broached with Teryk to all manner of customs, from interacting with the servants to handling interpersonal problems with other Fallen, and other such matters.

When she left about two hours later, she was glad Portia made her eat first. It seemed like this place would be livable—the rules made sense and weren't onerous. As soon as she was up to it, they'd send her on missions intended to investigate matters believed to relate to Reunion or actually relating to other Fallen or Fallen agents. Kelly knew nothing of what these missions were actually like, but Chavali would find out eventually, and there were other Fallen around to ask, like Portia.

Chapter 11

She slept poorly, her usual dreams replaced by confusing mish-mash she couldn't remember in the morning. They left her aching with loss, cringing with unease, panting and sweating. After that first full day, she spent a great deal of time in the study on her floor, looking through the books. Her grasp of written Shappan was minimal—aside from numbers, the clan didn't have much use for reading and writing and kept everything they truly needed orally. Deciphering a single page of text in many of the books was a time consuming chore, but luckily, some of them had interesting pictures.

Otherwise, she spent a few hours talking to Healer Kelly about inconsequential topics, just trying to get comfortable with the girl before moving on to broaching more serious ones. As for meals, she started alone but always found herself surrounded by people who engaged her in light chatter whether she wanted it or not, and they weren't even the same people. Apparently, it was required for Fallen to be overtly friendly to new people, and they all somehow knew every single Fallen by name. This made her put in effort to memorize names and faces, which she otherwise wouldn't bother to do.

On her fourth full day, as she climbed the stairs up from the twentieth floor, she nearly walked directly into Colby, his hands full with a tray of food. It was more her fault than his, though he wasn't paying as much attention as he could have. "Oh, hi, Chavali. How are you doing?"

"My complaints are few." The tray had an absolute mountain of food. "Is this really how much you eat in one meal?"

Colby laughed as he started going up again. "No, this is for two meals, two people. Most of it won't spoil for sitting out overnight."

"Ah," she nodded in understanding, "you have company for the night."

He got a faint blush, just a hint of pink on his tanned face. "Yeah, her five years are up in a few weeks. This is sort of celebrating."

It was heartening to know that Fallen actually lived that long. Not that she suspected this was a suicide mission overall, just that no one confirmed it prior to this. "Oh? What is she going to do then?"

"She's taking a position in the capital, with the government. I don't know what it is, so don't ask."

"No? Is it not serious, then, this thing you have?" Mostly, she was asking out of simple curiosity, to fill in details of the pictures here. As for the rest of her interest, it came from a desire to have as clear a map as possible of the connections between the many Fallen so as to avoid stupid social mistakes.

"No," he shrugged as much as the tray would allow. This was something he didn't like, he was attached to her. Was this the woman with the lips he wanted to forget, or was that someone else, from before his death? The latter was more likely than the former. "Well, there was a little bit of a thing, but not enough of one to hold her here. I guess this is really more of a goodbye thing than a celebrating thing."

"Not everyone has the wisdom to release what they cannot keep."

Colby's mouth drew down into a frown. "I don't really have a choice." He stopped on the steps, looking up, and sighed a little. "I'm not even sure what I'm doing. I like her, she's just—" Dropping his eyes back down, he looked at Chavali. "Why am I telling you this? I barely know you."

She gave him a sympathetic smile, one that was more fake than real, but the situation called for it. "Because I am here and listening. This counts for a great deal, I have noticed."

His frown softened and he started walking up again, she followed him. "Yeah. I just wish it all meant as much to her as it did to me."

This was starting to sound familiar, unpleasantly so. There was no possible way that his problems with this woman bore any real resemblance to her problems with Keino, but the underlying dynamic wasn't so different. Men could be such needy children. "There is no value in pining for what cannot be." If only she could truly take that lesson to heart herself. "But we all do it anyway."

He snorted in mild amusement. "I guess so." After a short pause, he asked, "Oh, how are you doing? The beginning is the hardest part and all."

There was no good answer to that, and she felt no compulsion to speak on any of it with him. "I will live."

"Glad to hear it." He smirked at her and nodded at the next doorway. "This is my stop. Have a good one."

Chavali nodded. "Good fortune to you. I hope it is not a difficult parting." She stopped and watched him acknowledge her well wishes, then walk down the hallway. Starting up again to her own floor, she stopped thinking about him and his stupid problems. She had plenty of her own to occupy her, and those of other people were irrelevant, except for how they affected her, and this one didn't.

Inside her own room, there was one of those problems. That basket still sat in the corner, as yet unopened. It was next to her bed. She sat down on that bed a short distance away, far enough she couldn't touch it without leaning over, and stared at it. There was no way to know what exactly was inside until she opened it, but somehow, leaving it there was more appealing. Until she opened it, anything could be in there. The mystery was what made it livable. She was sure the reality would be disappointing.

"Later," she told it, standing up and turning her back on it. "I will deal with you later. There are books to puzzle over now." Tossing a last look at it as she pulled her door not quite shut, she sighed, knowing she'd have to get to it eventually. She missed her clan, horribly, but was managing. Death wasn't a new thing, the clan lost people from time to time, due to age, harsh sickness, or argument with Outsiders. Usually, though, she saw the body. Usually, there was a ceremony. Usually, she had family around her still.

This was different. She didn't doubt what Eldrack said, not with what was happening when she died herself. It was still oddly surreal, like a nightmare she might wake up from. But that basket... She felt like as soon as she opened it, she would wake up and discover it wasn't a bad dream.

What was in there would be incontrovertible proof. Then, she would have to accept she was responsible for the entire clan in the form of her single person, and duty would demand she carry it on.

"Tomorrow," she told it firmly, then she turned her back and went to go try to read some more. Tomorrow turned to the next day, of course, then the next. Finally, eight days after she awoke from being dead, she sat on the floor, staring at her basket.

"You are just things." Her door was closed, no one would overhear this. "I'm not afraid of things. Not even things that remind me of Pasha or Keino." Chavali was proud of herself—she said both names without choking on them. "Or anyone else. You're my things, even, pieces of me from a different time that wasn't so long ago."

It still took her four deep breaths to move closer and pull the lid off. Even then, she didn't look immediately. She shut her eyes and took another few deep breaths before reaching in blindly and pulling something out. Cloth in her grasp, she looked at what was in her lap, finding her dress, the one she normally wore to play the part of fortune teller. It was a multi-layered garment that, when fully worn, left her neck and shoulders bare but covered everything else. It was in shades of brown from light to dark, with a reddish tint, much like her hair. The clothing was complicated to put on and take off, with small pieces of chain meant to dangle just so and lace cuffs that had to be arranged just so and laces that needed tying just so. Seer Marika wore something similar before her, but was slimmer—Chavali was built a little wider and more curvaceous, like her mother.

Blots of well dried blood marred the small lace detail of the front where it must have run down from her nose or eyes. The left sleeve, though, was clean, cleaner than the rest of the garment. Would she have any use at all for this dress here? Probably not. She was unclear on what sorts of duties she would have when they decided she had long enough to adjust, but wearing this thing struck her as unlikely to help her fulfill them. She shoved it aside and peered into the basket, now more confident she could handle the contents.

There was some other random clothing, none of it actually hers, but all of it recognizable as clan handiwork. A doll lay there, one she or Pasha probably made for a clan child, out of wood and corn husks, cloth and yarn, beads and string. She picked it up and brushed the yarn hair back, ran a finger over the bead eyes. Of all the things they could have rescued, it had to be this. Her eyes filled with tears as she imagined Pasha carefully pushing her needle through the head to secure the clump of yarn, slowly shaving strips off the sticks to make smooth arms for it, tying the string around the husks to form the body and dress.

This particular doll was well loved, but not worn. It, too, was cleaned, and she was almost positive this doll belonged to Haizea. Its eyes were the right shape, and it had that tiny scratch in the left arm. She hugged it to herself, trying to push away thoughts of how they must have found it next to the girl's broken little body, her eyes glassy and staring, covered with blood and ash. No, she had to focus on memories, on good memories. The girl was just one of many she knew since birth, but was the only one she had a piece of now. Everyone in the clan was similar enough that Haizea could be her own daughter, the one she never wanted to have herself.

It was a profanity against her clan that the children had been slaughtered. She was the clan now, making it an affront to her, personally. Somehow, someday, she was going to find that man and destroy him. She would take everything from him and then, if he was very, very lucky, she would kill him.

"I will avenge you," she vowed to the doll, then gently and reverently set it on the dresser.

Chapter 12

Chavali sat with Portia in the lounge, playing cards with two other women, Agatha and Violet. No one in the clan ever wanted to play with her, she was too good at bluffing and figuring out who else was bluffing. Pasha only agreed to play if it was for nothing, which meant they didn't really play cards so much as talk with props. Here, too, they were playing for nothing, just to pass the time in the company of others.

This was the second time she found herself drawn into such a thing, and she mostly stayed quiet the first time, still too raw to want to do otherwise. Now, though, halfway into the first hand, she had questions and wanted answers. "How many Fallen are there?"

"Oh, about a hundred and fifty or so," Portia answered casually. "Maybe a third are out on a mission at any given time. I think there's about twice that in Healers and servants." By now, she'd seen several of these servants—they worked in the kitchen, cleaned the washrooms, did the laundry, and kept everywhere neat and tidy. So far, she hadn't run into any in her room, but was sure someone swept her floor and dusted in there. They did not, however, make the exquisitely soft bed or pick up after her. It would be nice if someone explained the boundaries, but she was figuring them out anyway.

"This is all a big secret, so where do the servants come from? And where do they live?"

Agatha chuckled. She was a large woman, tall and muscle bound with long white hair always up in a tight bun. Chavali didn't really understand the point of having long hair if it was always up, but she didn't say anything about it. "Some of the servants are here with Fallen or Healers—spouses, siblings, dear friends. Some are from the village at the top. Some are former Fallen who didn't want to leave, but also didn't want to do the missions anymore. The ones that don't live with current Fallen have quarters down on some of the lower floors, where the kitchens and cafeteria are."

So, the Fallen had lives. They were not required to put everything on hold for five years, just some things. In truth, Chavali had no idea what she would do when her five years were up. The idea of being someone else's servant rankled, she wasn't interested in that. But, if she could stay in some other capacity, perhaps that would be the way to go. It was, so far as she could see, a nice place to live. Aside from the part where it was never moving.

"What of these missions? I have yet to be on one."

Portia opened her mouth, but a young man knocked on the door frame of the lounge. "Chavali? You're to report to Eldrack, I'll take you."

Instead of whatever she was going to say, Portia smiled in encouragement. "Looks like you're about to find out. Good luck."

Setting down her cards, Chavali gave the three women an apprehensive goodbye and followed the young man. He was about Pasha's age, but, as with every Outsider she ever met, looked nothing like clan. It was interesting, actually, that she never came across anyone that looked quite like clan. Granted, Estevior was supposed to have founded the clan twenty-five generations ago, and there were very few instances of Outsiders joining the clan, all early on, during Estevior's lifetime. Still, it was interesting.

They went down three floors, she counted them automatically already. This one, she hadn't done more than peer in at the doorway, it had nothing of particular interest so far as she could see. Apparently, though, it held the space Eldrack used for whatever this was about. The young man led her to a room with an open door and gave her a friendly smile she didn't return fast enough before he left her there. It was about the same size as her bedroom, roughly fifteen feet to a side, held a large round table with eight chairs and nothing else.

She stepped inside hesitantly, touching the back of the nearest chair, feeling rather like she was intruding in something but didn't know what that might be. After all, she was led here, shown to this place, by a servant who wouldn't have done so if he wasn't supposed to. Purposeful footsteps behind her made her look and pull her hand back as if she'd be scolded for touching something.

"Oh, hi." Colby was the one making those footsteps. He smiled at her and walked right in, chose a chair, and sat himself down in it. The wood groaned under his weight as he looked her over with a tactician's eye. He wore plain clothes, nothing special and no armor. His mouth opened a little as if he might say something else, but closed again as he apparently couldn't think of anything.

"Hello." Chavali watched him, face blank, trying to ignore that queer feeling he inspired, the one that made her want to apologize to him even though he was only being polite and sitting there. He wasn't clan, she had nothing to be sorry for. It wasn't her fault he had so many unpleasant things in his mind. She watched him ease back into the chair, looking fully comfortable here, like he knew exactly what to expect and for anything he didn't, he was certain he could handle and do a good job of it. She rather felt the opposite. It was incredibly annoying.

Silence sat between them, awkward and unpleasant like a child walking on ice for the first time. Casting her mind about for something to fill it, a memory tugged free, something she was ignoring for how disturbing it was at the time. "Fire," she said suddenly, the word almost a question, but too firm to truly be one. "You died in a fire. With children."

He shifted uncomfortably. "How did you know that?"

"I am a seer." She told Eldrack the truth, but was more hesitant to give it to anyone else. Even with Eldrack, she'd said only the barest minimum to avoid revealing secrets best kept close. Some things were not meant to be shared outside of the clan. At the sound of more footsteps coming their way, she shut her mouth. Wanting to avoid creating the wrong impression for whoever saw them, she slipped around the table to get farther from the door and sat in a chair not too close to Colby. That he watched her with confused suspicion didn't matter.

It was Eliot, with Eldrack and a new woman only a few steps behind him. Eliot paused in the doorway when he saw her, but only briefly. The way he looked her over quickly suggested he was apprehensive, but unsurprised to see her. Even so, he walked in and greeted Colby with a shake of his hand and clap on his arm. Had the other two not been right behind him, he likely would have started a conversation with Colby.

"I'm glad to see you found the room, Chavali." Eldrack gave everyone a warm smile, and the woman with him sat down in the chair beside his. One of her hands fiddled with a smoking pipe without knocking it on the table.

This new woman had an air of some authority about her, it sat lightly on her shoulders. Beyond that, her nose was crooked, there were scars across her face as if she ran into a plate of some kind and shattered it, her mouth seemed painted on by an idiot, and her jaw was square and mannish. Her hair was held back from her face by a wide strip of folded cloth—the dark, springy mass formed a ponytail at the back of her head. Each individual part was unappealing, but somehow, the whole formed a picture that Chavali felt she could stare at for hours to trace the intriguing lines with her eyes.

"This is Railan," Eldrack said, gesturing to the woman, waiting a moment while Chavali gave Railan a polite smile and received one in return. "You've already met Colby and Eliot." He set a folder on the desk without opening it, placed a hand on it to keep anyone from reaching for it. Before saying anything, he glanced at Railan, who lifted an eyebrow but said nothing. Eldrack sighed lightly and shook his head.

So, these two knew each other well, and had some kind of disagreement. Eldrack wasn't going to do it her way, no matter how right she thought she was. "All of you have something in common, which is exposure to Chavali's clan." He laced the fingers of both hands together on top of that folder. "Chavali, at least one other member of your clan may be alive."

"What?" She was stunned and blinked slowly. "You said..."

"I didn't lie to you." He glanced again at Railan, it was very brief. It was her idea not to tell Chavali this. "But we didn't have any real information. Just yesterday, we got some confirmation that a girl from your clan was taken to this—" He opened the folder and pushed it forward so they could actually see it. "-compound in the mountains and is very likely to still be there. I must emphasize that it's possible she's no longer there, or has not survived this long."

If there was another member of her clan, then it wasn't dead. She wasn't the end of it. With someone else, anyone else, it could go on. If it was a girl, that was all the better, because it meant Chavali wouldn't have to do anything she didn't want to. But more importantly, there was still someone to pass the stories to, still someone to bear children. They would start with-

Chavali's thoughts cut off as she noticed all four of them staring at her in silence. "Why did you not tell me?"

"Because there was nothing solid to go on." Railan finally spoke. Her words came out unhurried, in a kind of drawl too rough to place the accent of. She wasn't looking at Chavali, but at the pipe her fingers absently rolled between them. "There still isn't, not really. We're fairly certain the girl was taken there, but have no idea if she's been moved or not."

"Nothing...solid..." The words came out faintly; she didn't really mean to say them, her mouth just fell open and let them out. She snapped her jaws shut and let the anger that rose up from her belly spill over her. "This is my clan," she growled. "We are bound by Estevior's pact, our souls —" Cutting herself off, she crossed her arms and glared at the wall. That was a stupid thing to say, they had no right to know any of that.

"Who is Estevior?" Out of the corner of her eye, she saw Eldrack fix her with a look that made her want to slap him. It was sympathetic and friendly, nonthreatening. Railan was pretending not to be interested, examining her pipe still. The other two men looked uncomfortable, watching while trying not to stare.

Chavali ground her teeth a little and reached up to finger the pendant that wasn't there. This only served to further annoy her and she dropped the hand. "This is none of your business," she snapped.

Eldrack laced his fingers together again and nodded his understanding. "I haven't been completely honest with you, it's fair for you to be angry and return the favor." Again, a glance at Railan. He knew this would happen. "I didn't want to give you false hope. I still don't. He took two or three children, we know this with certainty. One of them is an older girl, the other one or two very young. There were no obvious clues where he took them. At least one of his men was a mercenary, we found the mark of his bonding, and have been following that trail ever since.

"By the time you woke up, Chavali, months passed. There is no way to be certain the children are still alive, or if they're at this location. They may not have been kept together. The reason he took them, I have no idea. Do you have any thoughts on that?"

"No," she snapped again. But now, her anger started to feel wild and unjustified. He wasn't trying to play her false, no matter how much she might want to think he was. These people were Outsiders, they didn't need to know anything. And yet, these people were giving her something of themselves, had already given her a treasure. Behaving like this, like protecting the clan was the most important thing, ever, full stop, felt cheap and even a little dirty. Childish. "Maybe."

She loosened a little but refused to look at any of them. "That man came for me because of the other gift I carry, the one all Seers of my clan have carried, for twenty-five generations, back to when the clan was founded. Estevior is the First Blaukenev, we know this." She sighed and rubbed the middle of her forehead wearily. "I know this. Much like my telepathy is uncontrolled, so, too, is my ability to predict the future, with accuracy." Her expectation was that this would surprise everyone present, at least partially. But it didn't. Only Colby and Eliot were stunned by the revelation, not Railan. Eldrack already knew, she remembered this from when she first awoke, though it wasn't clear to her at the time if he knew they were precise, uncontrolled. Somehow, he was fully aware of her 'gift'. He must have told Railan, but not the two men.

"He wanted control of this, and went there to take you." Finally looking up at her, Railan said this as if not reaching this conclusion was not thinking. "Why did he kill you, then?"

Chavali looked down at the table and reached a hand out to scrape at something on the surface that turned out to be an imperfection in the wood. Her fingernails were still painted. They hadn't chipped much yet, just a little bit on the thumb. Pasha did that, it was the last thing she had left of her sister. "He did not. I chose to kill myself to prevent him from having it. He was very...explicit about his intentions."

"Is it inherited?" Eliot sounded thoughtful, like this was just an interesting puzzle now. "Everyone in your clan looked a lot alike. Maybe he thought he was taking your little sister, or even your daughter."

Scowling, Chavali didn't answer right away. These people wanted to know everything. And while they were sitting here, trying to extract information from her, two or three of her clan's children were alone and scared, and had to be hurting from being apart from the Seer for so long. "What difference does it make why? He took them, that is what matters. Where is this place, and how long does it take to get there?"

Eldrack sighed and gestured to the folder, which Colby pulled toward himself and positioned so both he and Eliot could look it over. He, it seemed, gathered she wasn't going to say anything else. "It's not far from a Creator's Tower. Take supplies for a two day journey to be on the safe side. Given where it is, and what you'll be doing there, I wouldn't suggest taking mounts. Aside from Karias, that is."

Tucking her pipe into a small pouch on her belt, Railan spoke up. "The location is a small compound for the Order of the Strong Mind. That's an offshoot of the Strong Arm. I've been there, that's why we have the detail we do. This," she gestured to the folder, "is all several years old, though. Some things may have changed. It's important to keep in mind that they might not be aware of the circumstances the children were taken under. They might just think they've got some kind of mental potential and need to be trained."

Reading between those lines wasn't very hard—strong mind, mental potential. They were telepaths, likely the real thing. "Why should they not?" Chavali scoffed. "That man reached into my mind and took what he wanted."

"He..." Railan squinted at Chavali, apparently assuming she heard that incorrectly. "What? No one would do that."

"No, of course not," Chavali said sarcastically, then made a little noise of irritation. "He put his hand right in and left his filth behind. Those memories are tainted, I cannot think of them without feeling his slimy touch." Speaking of them naturally led to thinking of them, and she shivered, hugged herself.

"If you're not ready," Eldrack said gently, "you don't have to go. I thought it would be helpful for the children to see you, so they'd know it's safe to come along. But if you can't handle it yet, then you can't handle it yet."

It was a very tempting offer. Chavali sat there, trying to push those damned memories away, wishing she didn't agree that it would be better if she went. But if she didn't go, it would mean staying here, stuck underground and going nowhere. Though stagnation actually mattered very little to her, this was still a fundamentally different way to live. She was lonely, it was always too quiet. Even when she was with other people down here, she still had to speak Shappan, they still weren't clan, she still had to sleep by herself.

"I can handle this," she said softly, hoping for the words spoken aloud to convince her it was the truth.

"Then we should probably get going." Colby stood, making her feel very small. "I'll handle the supplies, Karias can carry plenty."

Eldrack also stood, leaving the folder there. "This is, of course, Chavali's first mission. Please keep that in mind."

Eliot stood as Eldrack left the room. "I'll meet you all in the tavern, then. I heard it's snowing again today." He and Colby walked out together with the folder, leaving Railan and Chavali still sitting at the table.

Chavali felt rather like she was being handed a wagon with no idea how to take care of it, deal with the horses, or even drive it. She would learn, yes, but someplace to start would be nice. The two of them sat there in a silence that felt strained and difficult to her, though Railan made no sign of breaking it anytime soon. For several minutes, they both just sat there, Chavali looking at her hands, Railan watching her.

It seemed like a very long time passed before Railan finally spoke. "Is there any chance you'll say more now all those men aren't around?"

"About my clan? No." Chavali had no interest in being poked and prodded on the subject, so she changed it. Meeting Railan's gaze somewhat defiantly, she said, "I have no idea what I am supposed to bring for something like this, though."

The other woman stood up. "Alright, then, let's get you geared up. If you normally use armor or weapons...?"

"No." Also standing, Chavali started for the door, Railan went with her. "I am a fortune teller and a storyteller, nothing more."

"Except that you experience accurate prophecies and are a limited telepath."

Eldrack must have explained to her how the telepathy works for her to apply 'limited' to it. "Neither is under my control."

"Right." Railan led the way up two floors and to a bedroom that Chavali supposed must be hers. It was the same as Chavali's, just with more things and a feel of actually being lived in. The rug on the floor caught her eye, mostly because she wouldn't mind having one herself. "What else can you do? Are you good at anything defensive, or punching people, or anything like that?"

Chavali made a face of distaste. "No. I had a bodyguard."

"Good to know." Railan picked up a small pack and set it on her table. Poking through it, she pulled a few things out, it looked like she normally kept more than she felt she would need. "That means you need to be protected and shouldn't be left alone." Picking the pack up again, she showed it to Chavali. "Most of us keep a bag ready to go all the time. I normally have mine set up for a week-long trip. Eldrack said two days, so I've got enough here—aside from food and water—for four days. Because something can always go horribly wrong. You were nomadic, right? So I probably don't need to help you pack?"

Chavali frowned. "We went in wagons. Other people handled such things. I am the Seer."

Grabbing a heavy cloak and trading her shoes for boots, Railan sighed a little. "Okay, so I do need to help you with that, then. Here's hoping those boys don't get bored waiting." She gestured for them to go.

"Eldrack is sending me *only* because these children are my clan." This was not a question. It did not escape her notice over the past week that everyone she met seemed to have skills that were more generally applicable to a variety of situations. Portia was a mage, Agatha had power at her command from her faith in the Order of the Feminine Divine, and she'd seen many people sparring competently.

Railan paused before answering. "It's not clear how useful you'll be in the field." She followed Chavali into her room and looked around. "Haven't really made it yours yet, I see."

"I have very little to do this with." Chavali went to her dresser and opened the drawers to pull clothes out.

Railan looked everything over, she seemed a little disapproving. "You haven't even gotten clothes of your own yet? Or do you actually like plain brown and white?"

"I cannot see color, it is not important to me." If she felt comfortable wearing the clothes from the basket, she would pull those out, but they felt like ghosts clung to them still. She laid things out on the bed, but really had very little, and had nothing to put it all into. "But no, I have not yet dealt with acquiring more. It did not seem particularly important."

Standing there with some consternation and disbelief on her face, Railan frowned, but just a tiny bit. "You know, you have a strange accent. I've never heard one like it before."

"It is of my clan." The comment had exactly nothing to do with packing, and Chavali wasn't sure what inspired it now. She knew everyone in her clan had an accent that marked them as strange to the rest of the world. They all knew this. Papá spoke the Outsiders' tongue as well as any Shappan yet still had the accent.

"Well, since I have empty space in my pack, we'll just stuff your clothes in with mine for now. When we get back, we'll get you properly equipped, and one of us will help you get some other things for your room. For now, we'll just get you winter clothes." Railan's hands were swift and sure, rolling up the clothing into tight little bundles that took up very little space.

Not long after, about a half hour after they left the small conference room, Chavali and Railan emerged in the tavern to find Eliot sitting at the bar with a steaming mug. He looked up when they entered, Chavali now in a heavy fur-lined cloak and boots with mittens, hat and scarf.

Railan, who dealt with those outfitter women there in her stead, told her everything but the fur—which was from rabbits and undyed—was a nice shade of red-brown that matched her hair.

"Did you have to stop to color coordinate?" Eliot was annoyed, but only marginally so.

"Yes, that's exactly what the holdup was," Railan said. She smiled at him like she dared him to press the issue.

Eliot rolled his eyes. "Let's go." He pushed his cup away and hopped to his feet. "We're meeting Colby at the stables." Without waiting for a response she didn't have, he pulled the door open and plunged into a light snowstorm. Tiny flakes fell swiftly, blowing around in wind not much stronger than a light breeze. It wasn't accumulating very fast, but it stung Chavali's eyes.

Though she didn't particularly want to, Chavali followed Eliot and Railan out. "Is it wise to leave in such a storm?"

Eliot shrugged. "Doesn't matter, we only have to get to the nearest Tower from here. If the weather was clear you'd be able to see it from here."

"I take it you didn't put up with this kind of weather much before?" Railan held the door open for her and shoved it shut when she was through.

"No, not really." Chavali pulled her hood up and her cloak shut. "We often traveled in the southern parts of Mecalle or South Cascain in the winter. When we did find ourselves farther north, I spent much time inside my family's wagon. I do remember one time we were camped in Grippa and much snow fell overnight. It took hours to dig the wagons out enough to move them, and even so, the road was difficult. I think we traveled only a few miles that day."

Eliot didn't seem amused or interested. Railan chuckled and might have said something, but the stable wasn't far, and they reached the large building quickly. Colby must have been watching for them, because he led his enormous horse out before they reached the door. This time, it was laden with saddlebags in addition to his saddle. No one particularly wanted to dawdle and they moved swiftly out of the small town. The three of them knew where they were going, Chavali just followed along. She adjusted her scarf so it covered much of her face and held her cloak over herself, yet she was still cold.

This was farther than Chavali had ever walked before. A half hour after they left, she was starting to feel it, in her feet and thighs, and her face was numb. They moved as a small group, which meant Railan walked with her, the two men behind them, and Chavali set the pace—slow but steady. Oddly, Colby didn't have to keep a tight lead on his horse as he walked beside it; the beast was more like an obedient dog than any horse she ever saw.

An hour into the walk, Chavali slowed down enough for Railan to notice. It was galling that they, all three of them, were able to walk long distances, were competent, could fight, could do things. "Are you alright?" The question was genuine, Railan really could tell something was wrong.

"I am not used to this much walking." No matter how much of a burden on her pride it was to admit this, if she didn't, she was going to fall over in the snow and have to be carried.

"Oh, here, you can ride Karias." Colby must have overheard the statement, it was hard for him not to. "I'll give you a hand up."

Chavali stopped and wasn't sure how to take the offer. Clearly, it was the best option here, but the horse was his, and he was sharing it with her for no reason other than that she was having difficulty. If he was clan, the offer wouldn't surprise her in the slightest. In actuality, if he was clan, she would have asked to ride in the first place. Standing here and freezing while they all stared at her wasn't helping anything, though. She nodded and took the hand up, found herself nearly tossed onto the back of the grey creature with white splotches.

"You can hold the reins if you want, but he'll follow me wherever I go unless I tell him not to." Colby handed the leather straps up to her.

"No," she shook her head and had to readjust her hood, "I do not need this. I am not much of a rider, either. We ride in the wagons." Up here, her head was at least ten feet off the ground, maybe more. Were it not for the refusal of the light snow to stop, she would have reveled in the height. Instead, she huddled in on herself, arranging the cloak so she could share the horse's body heat. It did not escape her notice that they picked up their pace quite a bit, walking much faster than she was comfortable with even at the beginning.

At this Creator's Tower, just like the rest, there was a small contingent of followers of the Order of the Creator's Path. They kept the Tower clean, the surrounding paths clear, and the travelers using them defended from any who might seek to cause trouble. For this service, they charged a small fee to use the Towers. It was curious this one didn't have a city around it, as in her experience, most of them did, but it was in the middle of the forest they just tromped through. Perhaps there was a sizable number of Order of the Pure Glade zealots here to keep the wilderness intact.

Colby helped her climb down from the horse as they approached the Tower. This was the first one she ever saw close up. It was about what she expected from seeing them at a distance: a five hundred foot tall obelisk of a single piece of glassy black rock with a giant pale blue crystal at the top that bathed the nearby area in its light. A wide archway at the foot let people inside, but they were stopped by two people in heavy armor and cloaks with swords and pikes, shields slung on one arm.

"Lovely weather," Railan said before either of them had a chance to speak. She held up her ring, the ring of the Fallen, so the guardians could see it.

One of them—it was impossible to tell gender, they were bundled up against the cold too much and the voice could be either—took her hand and looked the ring over. "Oh, yeah. We just love the cold. That's why we're stationed up here, you know: we can't get enough of nearly losing fingers to frostbite. Are you all on King's business, then?"

"Yep, traveling together." Railan smirked. "As if you don't recognize even one of us."

Uninterested in the exchange, Chavali looked around. It was beautiful, in its own way, and they'd done interesting things with the land around it—stones marked paths and spaces with rough shelters that might be intended for people to camp overnight. Also, she noticed there were archers in the nearby trees, and more of these armed people just inside. They probably had some kind of hidden living space nearby with more of them, too.

The guardians waved them through, they walked inside the relative shelter of the Tower. Curious, Chavali looked up. It was a hollow tube without stairs up, and the hole became narrower towards the top. They gathered into the circular beam of soft blue light cast down by the crystal. There was a rough map of the world on this side of the Creator's Divide on the floor with small blue crystal levers positioned to correspond to the other twenty-three Towers. Where this Tower's lever would be, which was on the east side of Shappa, there was instead a star etched in the floor.

Railan went directly to the northernmost one and pushed it down with with her foot. The blue light flashed, Chavali felt she was being pulled and twisted, dragged into something, then tossed away. The light faded back to that dim glow, and they were in a different place. It was not a pleasant experience, but it was vastly superior to walking for several days or weeks. Two more armored, cloaked figures, just like the previous two, stood outside, but it wasn't snowing here. The sky was still overcast, just without a storm moving through.

Without asking or being asked, Colby helped Chavali back up onto the horse, then the group set a ground devouring pace to the east and a little south, into the mountains. This Tower was in the foothills of the range between Shappa and Grippa, north of a large forest. From here, the north coast wasn't visible, it was still too far away. The terrain gradually got rougher, the light started to fade away. When it was near dark, Railan stopped at the crest of a hill.

"We're almost there. I recognize where we are, it should be just over that next rise."

Colby looked off into the distance where Railan pointed. Their backs were to Chavali still up on the horse, so she could only guess what might be going through their heads. "It's been a pretty long day, and I don't think darkness will help us much. Since we all need light to see by, I expect it'll really only hinder. We should look for a place to camp and start in first thing in the morning. Provided it doesn't take too long to get in and out, we should be able to get back tomorrow night."

It was interesting that Colby acted like he was in charge, even though Chavali got the distinct impression Railan and Eliot had both been around longer. Eliot nodded as he, too, stared off in that direction. "I agree. Let's find someplace to camp." He leaned closer and muttered something, Chavali had the distinct impression it was about her. She could guess it was disparaging, probably about her lack of skills.

Railan pointed down the slope at her feet. "I think that's an overhang, we can maybe get some shelter under it."

Without waiting to be told or helped, Chavali did her best to climb down from the horse. It was easier than getting up, though not if her goal was to be graceful. She fell farther than she meant to and only avoided landing on her bottom by virtue of a tight grip on the saddle. The horse turned his head to look at her, and she could swear she saw his eyes light up with laughter. Stupid horse. No one else paid her less than impressive dismount any attention, they just began forging down the hill.

Thank goodness for the mittens, because otherwise, her hands would've been cut up by the rocks she kept leaning on and grabbing as she moved down the steep slope. It wasn't very far until she was on a flat space with the others, the horse coming down behind her. A slab of rock jutted out about five feet above, offering something of a shelter. The horse didn't fit under it and Colby couldn't come close to standing, but Railan, Eliot, and Chavali only had to bend over a little.

"Karias can block this side most of the way," Colby offered. In response to the statement, the horse did just that, clopping to the side and getting down on the ground. His massive girth nearly took up the whole edge, and he leaned his head down so it was partially under the rock. It didn't look to Chavali like Colby gave the horse any commands to make Karias do that, other than suggesting it out loud, though no one else gave the action a second glance.

"He is very well trained," Chavali observed.

Colby didn't answer, he just bent to the task of pulling the saddle-bags off the horse and rummaging through them for things.

"I guess you probably don't know how to cook anything?" Eliot was clearly tiring of her incompetence.

To be fair, so was Chavali. "No, but I know how to entertain weary travelers." She sat down where she could lean against the horse and curled up on herself, but pulled her mittens off. The air was much too cold to leave them off for long, but they made it difficult to twine her fingers through the spirits. Her hands danced through the air to produce images of four goats.

Eliot watched, but turned his attention to his pack when he saw what she made. "I think we've already heard that story."

"I use the four goats for many stories. They are not like people but are familiar to the children." She slipped her mittens back on. No need for her fingers to freeze once the images were created.

Colby coughed lightly. "I seem to remember that little girl in your lap suggested the goats should spend their time with sex. I suppose it makes sense, I've just never heard a child that young say something like that."

Grinning, Chavali nodded. "We do not have separate wagons for everyone—two hundred and thirty-one people travel in forty-two wagons, and we group by family." Her face fell. "Traveled. Grouped." Shaking her head to fling aside memories, she reached for what she spoke of before. "My sister was seven years younger than me. It was not for lack of trying on the part of my parents. I had an older brother, too, and he had a wife. They also had been enthusiastically trying to have children for a few years. We all, the six of us, slept in one wagon, in one bed. No one bothered to sneak off for sex, they just covered themselves with a blanket. Zuli, my brother's wife, could be rather loud. Sometimes, my mother would reach over and smack her to shut her up so the rest of us could sleep."

Eliot found this funny, Colby blushed as he shook his head in mild amusement, Railan looked entertained. "That's certainly different from the way most other people do things," Railan said with a light snort. She pulled out her pipe, stuffed it with something, and tapped it on the bottom while focusing on it. Within seconds, it started producing a small amount of scented smoke—it seemed citrusy and thankfully didn't waft in anyone's face.

"I have seen this. For others, it is a private thing, and I understand. We do not prance about naked or bed each other without a connection, but there is no practical way to have the degree of privacy one does when you live in a house with rooms. I expect the very poor are the same, the ones who have only small hovels or less." Chavali took a cup of water passed to her by Railan, and sipped at it while Colby set to the task of starting a fire with some scavenged wood.

"I do not normally speak in great detail about the subject with young children, I only explain the basics. Some are concerned about the noises and only wish to be sure their parents are not hurting each other. All are curious about the point and particulars of it." She shrugged, wishing the water was hot tea. It was already cool enough to make her insides feel chilled for drinking it. The illusionary goats moved out of the way, she had them graze on nonexistent grass just for the familiarity of it.

Colby was definitely sorry he brought the subject up. "Does anyone object to a cold meal? Nothing is willing to catch fire right now."

"That's probably for the best," Eliot said with a light shrug. "That much smoke and light would only give us away anyway." He took the apple Colby handed him as a start to the meal, and lightly tossed it from one hand to the other. "We should discuss what we're going to do when we reach it."

"I can't see any way we'll just convince them to give the kids to us." Railan took an apple, also, rubbed it on her cloak as she puffed on the pipe. "Not from the outside, anyway. We'll have to break in and steal them."

Eliot shrugged. "Pretend like they're wiggly statues we need to recover. Only better, because at least one can walk."

Before Chavali could be overly annoyed by that comment, Colby handed her an apple and looked at her squarely. "How do you think they'll handle the idea of being quiet and sneaking out?"

Looking down at the apple, turning it over in her hands, Chavali thought about it. "If they have been treated well, they may be confused, but I believe they will do whatever I tell them to as much as they are able. If I can have a minute to speak with them, it should not be a problem." She closed her eyes, trying to still the excitement and foreboding. She was getting some of her clan back, but had no idea of their condition.

The crunching of apples and Railan's smoke filled the space for a short time, Colby also handed out cheese and biscuits that were only a little smashed for having been packed. That seemed to be the end of the tactical discussion, though Chavali wasn't sure what they hoped to accomplish with only this much determined ahead of time. While she didn't have any idea how to go about breaking into a place to take something, it seemed to her that the planning ought to be at least a little more intensive than that short conversation. Her own role was reasonably defined, though, which made it difficult for her to grasp what sorts of questions would be useful instead of a waste of time.

When she was done with the food, which didn't do much to warm her but did fill her belly, she watched the four illusory goats on their illusory grass, doing nothing but ordinary goat things. Like this, she could almost imagine she was home with her clan, sitting out in the cold because she had to for some reason. All it took to dispel the fantasy was Eliot moving so he could stand up. One glance at him—which she did because the movement attracted her eye—reminded her forcefully she was not with clan.

It took nothing from her to keep the goats going while she could still see them, but she waved her hand to banish it as the others pulled out blankets and made what pillows they could from other things. She stayed where she was while they chose places to lie down, not sure how to fit herself into this sort of thing. Railan handed her a blanket, she took it with a grateful nod, but still waited. For what, she wasn't sure, because even they were settled, she still sat there.

"I guess you've never slept on the ground?" Colby smiled sympathetically as she shook her head. "It's not so bad when you get used to it." He patted the horse's flank lightly, he was covered with a blanket now. "Karias won't mind if you lean on him."

Whether he meant it as a true invitation or not, Chavali got up and stepped over next to him, settling herself with Karias and Colby forming a corner for her. They were both covered up so completely she had no fear of his dreams invading her own. He, however, was surprised to have her cozying up to him. It was in how his body suddenly tensed, how he made a little noise of mild dismay, how he moved his arm awkwardly. Even so, he must not have objected much, because a few seconds after she stopped squirming around to find as comfortable a spot as she could, he relaxed and didn't shove her away.

Chapter 13

In the morning, Chavali woke up because the bodies under hers stirred. She found herself warm and draped across Colby's broad chest, Railan just stretching where she was curled up next to Chavali's legs. Eliot was at her back. One of Colby's large hands absently stroked her hair, but he managed to avoid touching her skin. Pushing herself up, she startled his hand away—he pulled it from her quickly, like he'd been caught doing something he shouldn't.

"Good morning," Chavali got out around a yawn. The sky cleared overnight, the sun was just announcing itself with a dim orange glow coming from behind the mountains. She rolled her neck around, it was a little stiff. "You are a good pillow," she told Colby with a weary grin.

"Thanks, I think." Colby chuckled lightly as he carefully levered himself out from under the overhang. "I think if we leave Karias there," he pointed at a spot in the distance, "as a rally point, that should work out well. He'll be an unexpected defender if we manage to acquire pursuit." As an afterthought, he turned and crouched down, looking at Chavali. "How are you at running for your life?" The question was more than half jest, but not completely.

Chavali lifted an eyebrow. "I am more used to being defended. It is worth saying that this girl, the older one, is capable of some self-defense. We teach them to use weapons from an early age."

"Interesting," Eliot said as he stood and stretched his back, making it crack loudly. "Why aren't you capable of it, then?"

"I was chosen for my position when I was five. I did not have time for such things. No one was certain when Marika, my predecessor, would die, so I had to be ready to take over as soon as possible. I acted as her assistant when she did fortune telling from the age of ten. Probably, I would have been asked to choose my successor in the next few years from the young girls." Haizea would have been her choice. The girl was sharp.

Railan collected things instead of stretching, and Chavali did her best to help with that chore. After another fifteen minutes or so of tending to morning needs, the group got underway, eating a small meal on foot. Despite soreness all over about which she refused to complain, Chavali rode again. She thought perhaps Colby was gentler with her as he helped her up, but it might have been just that he suspected she would be in poor shape. It took them half an hour to reach the point where Colby wanted to leave Karias. Chavali had to walk from there.

They paused in hiding just before the crest of the last rocky rise where they could see the small compound below them, nestled in a flat space. "It goes into the side of the mountain," Railan said quietly, "in and down. What we're seeing is maybe a quarter of the facility. If we circle around, we should be able to climb that wall and get inside without anyone noticing."

Where she pointed looked a lot like a sheer rock face to Chavali.

"You want to climb that? Are you mad?"

Eliot snorted in amusement. "I'm going to scale it. You're going to use the rope I drop down from the top."

"Correction," Railan tossed out, "we—you and I—are going to scale it. I need to be there to keep any passive scans from detecting your mind. We're about to break into a place run by telepaths. It's protected from unwanted minds as much as bodies. Don't worry," she smirked at his skeptical look, "I'm probably better at climbing than you are."

"That's a good place for Chavali and I to wait for a signal." Colby pointed at a spot that didn't look too hard to get into, but wasn't so close they'd be in danger of alerting anyone who might happen to look that way.

It took the four of them another half hour to reach Colby's chosen waiting spot, then Railan and Eliot went on without them. For a short time, both lay silently on the ground watching the other two run the rest of the way to the wall. The climbing part looked like it was going to take some time. "Why did Eldrack send you to my clan?"

Colby let out a heavy breath. "If he hasn't told you, I probably shouldn't, either."

"Is this how it is to be Fallen? Always when you ask a question, it is up to Eldrack?"

"You haven't exactly been forthcoming with answers yourself."

"You have been Fallen for...four months, maybe five now? You hold to their secrets well enough already. I have been clan for twenty-five winters. How well do you think I hold our secrets?"

Colby paused, thinking that over. Both of them still watched the two climbers, making progress up the wall. "He told us your clan was an oddity. No one else in all the world does what you do, or behaves the way you do. He asked us to see if we could get you to tell us any stories about the past of the clan, ones that might point to why you are the way you are. I got the impression we weren't the first to have a look at your clan, just the first Fallen to specifically go and try to get something on purpose."

Chavali nodded, her suspicions now confirmed. "I knew it was something like this. That you found us on purpose, that it was the clan you were interested in."

"Really?" Colby turned to regard her, looked her over more appraisingly. "You could tell that much?"

"I knew this when you first rode past the wagons on the road. Had I not seen the memories of your death, I would have learned more that night, possibly discovered the secret of the Fallen. What an interesting possibility that is."

"What, exactly, did you see of my death?"

Chavali shrugged. "It was very confusing. Your memory of dying made no sense because you are alive. Everything else was tainted by that, and it was all very fast as you wracked your mind for a question to ask me."

"I wish I'd known you were in my thoughts."

She snorted. "If I told people this is how I tell their fortunes, I would not make any money doing it."

"Your entire job was lying to people." The way he said that, it was a kind of disappointment, something he thought was sad and pathetic and wrong.

"I sold to people what their minds told me they wanted to hear. In some cases, it was more what they needed to hear." She shrugged, not remotely conflicted. "People want to believe in things greater than them-selves, that they are important to forces they cannot understand."

"The Creator isn't just a tale we tell ourselves to feel better, Chavali," he chided, "she's real."

As it always did, a full force assertion of the Creator's existence made her uncomfortable. There was something about it being stated flatly that bothered her, though she could never pin down what it was. "And yet, she is not particularly interested in the little parts of anyone's life, no mat-ter what we think or wish."

Colby was quiet for a short time again, his eyes back on the two climbers. "You sound like you don't actually care much what the Greatest Sin is. I remember you saying something about it being stagnation."

"The subject is not one I consider particularly critical to my life. What of you, though?"

"I happen to think it's lying. Being dishonest, especially to oneself."

No wonder he behaved like that, then. She smirked and let out a huff of amusement. "I must be the most abhorrent creature imaginable to you. How have you managed to reconcile the need to keep secrets with this idea?"

He glanced at her briefly. "I've found ways to be honest without revealing them. We are an Order, in a sense, for example, and I have no problem telling people I belong to one."

"I see." She smirked, but didn't tell him what she thought of that. If he wanted to believe that was honesty, she wasn't going to burst his little bubble. Not at this point, anyway. There was nothing to be gained by throwing him off balance right now. In fact, it might endanger the children if she did.

"There's the signal," Colby said as he got to his feet and helped her up. They scrambled quickly across the slope together, him making sure she didn't fall, her trying not to get tangled up in her cloak and skirts. By the time they reached the wall, a rope dangled down. Colby hurriedly tied a loop at the end. "When I'm up, put your foot in that and hold on tightly, we'll pull you up."

He swarmed up the rope quickly. She did as he instructed and was pulled up just as swiftly. At the top, the jump down to the other side wasn't bad. Colby caught her so she didn't hurt herself, and she actually liked that a little more than she wanted to. His hands were strong and certain, and she was reminded of Keino in that moment. Except that Colby let her go and demanded nothing from her, which made him a vast improvement.

From there, in order for Railan to protect them all, they had to stay together. Chavali moved as quietly as she could—it was better than Colby could do in his metal armor. They were in a garden, slipped through it to a side door. Eliot crouched at the door with some tools for a short time. It clicked open and they slipped inside, where Railan took the lead. Feeling as though it might matter, Chavali pulled her mittens off and stuffed them in a pocket. It was warm enough she didn't really need the cloak, but all she did was pull her hood down. If she took the whole thing off, she'd just have to carry it. Better to leave it on her shoulders than to have to put up with it draped over an arm or balled up in a fist.

Within a minute or two, they came across someone, a woman in loose robes with the weight of several decades on her. She squinted at

Railan, frowning. "Is that you, Tanith?" As the woman came a little closer, Chavali saw her eyes were filmy, a light white mist covering them over. Likely, she could still see a little, but everything must be indistinct and hazy.

She strode forward and took the old woman's outstretched hand. "No, not Tanith," she said kindly. From her mind, Chavali knew several things immediately, and wanted to extract more. "I am new here, and lost." The effort to temper her accent so she sounded more like it was Grippan made her have to choose her words carefully, but it was the closest to her own. "Yvette, right? Harris told me about you. He said to go tend to the children, but I am missing my way."

"Oh, you poor dear." Yvette patted her hand kindly. Chavali sensed the words before they came out of the woman's mouth, but waited until they were actually spoken. There was more, too, and she was tempted to nurture the seeds of distrust she found. "They're in the second basement. A dreadful place to keep children, but," she leaned in conspiratorially, "I've heard they're a little dangerous somehow."

It was freeing to not have to worry about faking her facial expressions, but she still controlled her voice carefully. "You have heard? Does not anyone tell you things directly? I would have thought someone as experienced as you would be important enough here to know everything that happens."

Yvette smiled. *Child, if only that was the case.* "I can't do as much as I once could."

"You seem perfectly capable to me." Carefully making herself sound indignant, she squeezed the woman's hand. "I was taught to respect my elders, to learn at their knee, to attend their wisdom.”

"You're a dear," Yvette said, her smile brighter now. "I don't want to keep you from what you're supposed to be doing, though. I wouldn't want you to get into trouble." *Harris is an ass, he'll punish you harshly.* "Come by and see me later, when you have some free time." She patted Chavali's hand again and let her go, puttered off without noticing the rest of the group.

"I will," Chavali promised to her back. It was somewhat annoying to discover a person here who deserved nothing in retribution. Even with Railan's warning to that effect, she still had the notion everyone here would turn out to be fully complicit in whatever was being done to the children. This was not the case, and it made the mission seem more complex for it.

As soon as the woman was out of earshot, Railan hissed out, "Good work. Down we go."

Not so useless after all. Chavali let Railan and Eliot get ahead of her before starting to walk again, Colby following her and paying attention behind them. Perhaps he was the one who would wind up being useless, as swordplay didn't seem terribly likely here. Railan took them through this level of living quarters and kitchens, following an odd, winding path. The reason for the roundabout route wasn't clear until she made them hug the wall near a corner with a gesture.

Two men walked past the opening of the hallway, too intent on their destination to notice four people lurking off to the side. She had to be taking them around the denizens, sensing them and avoiding the spots they'd most easily be seen. They waited until those two men were well gone before slipping across the hall and finally finding the stairs. Going down, they passed a man that Railan nodded to, choosing the approach of looking like they belonged.

Everything was fine until he saw Chavali. The man stopped while she kept going, and he turned to stare at her. "You...you're..." He frowned with confusion and shook his head a little. "Who are you?"

Before she could do more than turn to look, Colby put his large hand on the man's head and slammed it against the wall, hard enough to knock him unconscious, but not hard enough to smash his skull. The efficiency was startling, and Chavali flinched away. Eliot, though, hurried back up and checked the man over.

"Leave him or kill him?" His voice was quiet, the question whispered.

"Leave him," Colby whispered back. "They'll know we were here as soon as they notice the children missing."

Eliot and Railan both nodded their agreement and moved with more haste. Now, they only had until this man woke up or was found. By then, they needed to be away from here, far enough to avoid detection. It seemed an avoidable complication to Chavali. She looked back at Colby with a scowl and whispered harshly, "I could have—"

"No time for that," Colby put a hand on her shoulder and turned her around, pushed her to get her to moving again. She threw a venomous glare over her shoulder, but he wasn't looking, making it less satisfying. At the next floor, Railan and Eliot flanked the doorway and peered through while Chavali and Colby stayed back. Why Railan didn't just do whatever she was doing upstairs was a mystery, but Chavali wasn't about to question it.

They flitted out the doorway and into an intersection of stone hall-ways lit by an insufficient number of flickering torches, choosing one and hurrying up it. Here, they weren't sure which room exactly and started opening doors, peering inside. The first one bothered Chavali immensely. These were cells, obviously meant to hold unwilling subjects. A lock with no way to unlock it from the inside was disturbing enough on its own, but there were also chains in the walls. It had nothing like a cushion to sleep or even sit on, no windows—nothing appropriate for children by any stretch of the imagination.

Voices drifted around down here, wordless echoes of people speak-ing far enough away or muffled enough to be indistinct. It had to be designed to drive a listener mad. Chavali tried to ignore them, but her mind wanted to latch onto them and find words, meanings, something, any-thing. The spirits she was bound to reached for them also, wanted to answer them. Their voices added to the ones outside her head, also too vague to be understood, and she wanted to scream at whoever was down here to shut up.

The only way it seemed possible to make it all stop was to screw her eyes shut and cover her ears, but that didn't help. Colby patted her shoul-der to get her attention, she opened her eyes to see him looking down at her with concern. He pointed, she followed that finger with her gaze to see Eliot glaring at her impatiently, Railan watching her impassively. "What do you hear?" Railan hissed.

"Voices. I cannot make them out or shut them off. It is madden-ing."

"Huh." Railan reached over and put a firm hand on Chavali's shoulder, squeezed it lightly. "You're sensitive. That's interesting." At least she knew she wasn't going insane. Small comfort, that. For a moment, it looked like Railan was going to launch into an explanation, but her eyes flicked to Colby and back. "We'll talk about it later. Just try to focus on why we're here. Colby, if she stops like that again, pick her up. They're doing something down here I think she's picking up on, and she's not shielded, and it's not anything pleasant."

Eliot rolled his eyes in annoyance, but said nothing and started moving again. Railan squeezed her shoulder again and let go, went back to getting them through this mess. If whatever they were doing wasn't pleasant and was being done to her clan, she wanted them—whoever they might be—dead as soon as possible, preferably painfully. If it was that man, she wasn't sure how that would happen, but she felt confident at least one of them could think of something.

Walking towards the source of the whispering didn't make anything clearer, but it did make it harder for her to think. She covered her ears again and quickly found herself slung over Colby's shoulder. It freed her to concentrate on shutting that noise out, though she didn't succeed. In some ways, it was worse, because she had nothing else to distract her from the noise.

Colby stopped. She was set down with her back to the nearest wall, where she slid down it to sit on the floor and curled up in a ball. The voices were loud, oppressive, and still she couldn't understand them. This wasn't worse than the pain of a prophecy, it was just different. So different, she didn't know how to cope with it. Holding her head, she rocked on her heels. She thought she heard the sound of a door being smashed open.

The voices stopped abruptly. When she looked up to see what happened, she wasn't in a dank stone corridor anymore. Instead, she stood in a meadow, four goats grazing nearby. Everything was in color, saturated with it to the point of being the epitomes of those colors, to the point of being obviously fake. Yet, when she bent enough to run her hand over the top of the very green grass and very yellow and pink flowers, it felt very real. She hadn't seen colors for ten years, aside from purple for the prophecies, but that wasn't the same.

It was like smelling something she forgot she liked and being surprised to discover she still liked it. This was how she imagined Auivel's tea would taste if she could find some now. Plucking a pink flower, she lifted it and stared at it, determined to memorize how the color looked. Her fingernails were still painted, and the flower matched them perfectly. She pulled the locks of her hair with the beads in them, saw the colors of them for the first time: shades of pink and red that leaned toward brown. Her hair was darker than she remembered, had more red in it.

Whatever this place was, she never wanted to leave. She was warm and comfortable, there was no one around to remind her of how useless she was now, how little she could contribute to her new clan. It was, perhaps, a little lonely, but there were goats. Over there, she saw a plant with zucchini growing on it. Another group of plants had beans on them. With that and the goats, she wasn't going to starve. This place had everything! It was perfect.

She spun around, reveling in the colors, the sweet scent of the flowers, the sun on her skin, the quiet buzzing of bumblebees. That she knew it was winter right now didn't matter. That she knew they were doing something important right now didn't matter. That she knew this wasn't possible didn't matter right now. Running over to the goats, she hugged the nearest one, ruffled the hair on its head affectionately.

Animals had thoughts, they were just less organized, less coherent, less complex. Whenever a horse was cranky and no one could figure out why, Chavali would put a hand on it and be pointed directly at the thing bothering it. She didn't particularly enjoy delving into their minds; it was like being dragged behind a wagon by her foot. Smaller animals had smaller minds, and she got nothing from creatures smaller than a cat or so, there wasn't enough for the spirits to latch onto. Or so she surmised—there might be some other reason.

This goat had no thoughts at all. Her hand rested on it, which should be enough, but she got nothing, not even a sense of satisfaction about eating the grass. She could feel the goat, it was warm, the hair was exactly as coarse as it should be. She could hear the goat as it chewed and swallowed, then ripped up a new mouthful of grass. She could smell the goat, it had the usual animal odor mixed with earth. And yet, she couldn't sense its mind at all, not even when she made the effort to be touching its skin instead of just its hair.

Backing off from it, she tripped and fell, hit the ground heavily. That hurt, just like it was supposed to. What did all of this mean? Did someone take the spirits from her? Without her noticing. In a split second. While throwing her into some kind of fantasy place. As preposterous as that explanation was, she couldn't think of another. What was she supposed to be doing again?

Clan. She was here for clan, for Blaukenevs, lost and alone, left without their Seer. She was here to bring them to whatever she could make of a home for them. Children, they were children. This was a rescue, and they were important. These children were the most important thing imaginable, and that she forgot about them for even a second was proof in itself of how false this place was. How long was she here, how much time did she waste being 'happy'?

Never mind that, it wasn't important. What mattered now was finding a way out, a way to get back to clan, to home, to sanity. She surged to her feet, looked all around. It was an endless meadow, no matter where she looked, with a wide blue sky and a sun. What could she reach? In case it was only a little past her head, she jumped up, waving her hands, but touched nothing. If she couldn't reach the sky, what else was there?

The ground, stupid. She dropped to her knees and felt around, trying to find a crack or soft spot, or anything, but it was all seamless, all...covered in grass. She began ripping out fistfuls of grass, tossing it all around. Under the grass was dirt, but she didn't give up. "I know this isn't real," she snarled at the dirt as she dug into it with her painted fingernails and flung the dark earth away. "Do I wish I could see colors again? Yes. Of course. I miss that every single day. If it isn't missed, you freehanded scapegrace, it's not a sacrifice. I gave that up willingly, though. I knew it was going to happen and I didn't flinch. Because this duty is the pride and honor of my clan, and I will never surrender it, not even in a fantasy."

As she flung words at the ground, she pawed at it with growing intensity. "This is my clan you're messing with, and it's my mind, and you will not have either! I will defy you with my every breath, even the last if need be." Her hands scraped something, it wasn't dirt and left sharp stings on her fingers. Surprised, she yanked her hands up and looked them over, to find cuts with blood welling up. "This is not real," she growled, and set back to the task, scraping more of the dirt away until she found pink tinted crystals sticking up, sharp little knives cutting into her hands, shredding her fingers.

The pain reminded her of her death, of slamming that small blade into her wrist and yanking it out again. It felt quite the same, in fact, so much so that she suspected her mind was just conjuring it as the most recent trauma of this type and magnitude. She wasn't getting anywhere, though, now that the dirt was gone. Except the crystals were changing from light pink to darker pink, and the darker they got, the more brittle they became. Her blood was staining them, eating away at them.

She froze with this realization, uncertainty taking hold. If she bled herself out in this, would she die? There would be no third chance, this much was made clear to her. Only once could a person be brought back, and only then with a great cost. Portia explained this, she had no reason to doubt its truth. But no other way to get out presented itself. If they were all trapped somehow, and the others couldn't figure a way out, couldn't fight their way clear of the complacency the place inspired, then it was up to her to do something. Her clan needed at least one of them to survive and get them to safety.

Taking one deep breath to steel herself, then another, she scraped both arms over the crystals and left them there, gritting her teeth as her blood pumped out, darkening the crystals swiftly. Before she lost feeling in them, she pushed down, leaning her weight on it. She fell, head first.

Chapter 14

Sucking in a breath, Chavali opened her eyes. She was back in that stone corridor, the door smashed open, the color gone from everything. Colby and Eliot lay on the floor with her, staring off at nothing. Both men were alive, but must be trapped in a similar sort of dreamscape as she was. Railan was down on one knee, facing the room, her hands held out in front of her as if to ward off an assailant. Even from behind, Chavali could see the woman was under a great deal of strain.

Inside the room, two men sat in wooden chairs. They hadn't even gotten up. Their eyes were closed, both of them faced Railan and they, too, were concentrating. For them, it wasn't nearly so difficult as for Railan. No wonder, two against one was hardly a fair fight. Beyond the two of them, she saw a figure huddled in the corner, face hidden. All she could see of the child—this had to be the older one, as she wasn't much smaller than Chavali herself—was dark hair long enough to mark her as a girl.

Clan. Even though she couldn't say who it was, this girl was clan, and she was not going to let clan go again without a fight. Her thoughts were clear but simple as she grabbed the closest weapon she could find, one of Eliot's swords. Getting off the floor, she walked right up to the two men and stood there for a moment, uncertain how exactly to use the blade. Neither of them noticed her; they were unaware she broke free of their trap.

Hefting the blade, she looked down at it, then at the man on the left, back to the blade. Would he scream? How long would it take for the pain to end and his life to drain away? Was this the right thing to do? Yes, they harmed clan, but she never did anything worse to anyone than slap Keino across the face, tell people they were idiots. If Keino was here now, he wouldn't hesitate. Because that girl was clan, and these men were doing something to her.

She shoved the blade into his neck. It seemed the easiest way to be sure he wouldn't survive the blow long without worrying about a bone getting in the way, and it would keep him from crying out. It hit his spine, he opened his eyes and his mouth and stared in shock as he gasped and clutched at his throat and slumped and slid off the chair. Not expecting the movement, the spray of blood, any of it, the blade went with him, pulled from her hands.

Behind her, Railan let out a groan. The other man squeaked and opened his eyes. Too stunned by her own actions to do anything coherent, Chavali didn't watch what happened to him, she just rushed for the girl and gathered her up in her arms. "I'm here," she told the girl softly. "You're safe." She vaguely heard a queer popping sound behind her. Railan grunted, then panted. Other noises a little further away announced the two men waking from their dreams and getting up. The three of them spoke in hushed voices.

Chavali pulled back enough to see who she just rescued. "Biholtz," she said, not stifling tears as she brushed the girl's face and shared her relief.

Biholtz couldn't make words come from her mouth, but Chavali could tell how joyful the girl was to see her anyway.

"Chavali," Eliot said softly, his hand lightly touching her shoulder, "we can't stay here like this." He sounded a great deal less annoyed with Chavali than he'd been so far. In fact, she thought he almost respected her now.

Though Biholtz needed the embrace and reassurance, Chavali pulled away from her enough to look her in the eyes, her hands on the girl's cheeks to hold her face steady. "Are there others here?" To damnation with the rules, she spoke the clan tongue in front of Eliot.

"Yes," Biholtz nodded, sniffling. "Haizea and Danel. They said if I didn't cooperate, they'd hurt them. They're here, if I'm good they let me see one or the other."

"We have to find them and take them with us. Do you know where they are?"

Biholtz shook her head and stood with Chavali's help. "They always brought them to me. I didn't go to them." Her eyes drifted down and she sucked in a breath. "You've got blood all over..." Sweeping her gaze across the room, her eyes went wide and her mouth opened and shut a little. For good reason, Chavali noted as she also surveyed the carnage.

There was her own handiwork, his head now completely severed and the blade back in Eliot's hand. He stood with Colby and Railan, tucking things into pockets. Colby supported Railan, who dropped with exhaustion. The other man was more gruesome, in a way. His face was blown wide open, as if his eyes exploded outwards. Things that belonged on the inside hung oddly and dribbled out, but his mouth still formed a grimace of pain.

"Don't look at that," Chavali said forcefully, pulling Biholtz in close to bury the girl's face in her neck. "Step over this one, and we're leaving the room." Switching to Shappan, she told the group of three, "There are two more, small ones, a boy and a girl. She does not know where they are, just that they are here, used to keep her behaving." Outside the room, she pulled her cloak off and wrapped it around the girl's shoulders.

Colby's face contorted with rage, Eliot's drew down with disapproval. Railan was still exhausted, but stood up straight, held her head high, and said, "We're not leaving them here. I'm not going to be much more use, though. Those two took a lot out of me. A little longer and they would've overpowered me."

"One of you," Chavali indicated Eliot and Colby, "should start getting her out, then, I think. The other comes with Biholtz and me, we will find them and may need to leave swiftly."

No one liked this plan, but Colby nodded his grudging acceptance. "She's right. You can't make it out on your own," he told Railan, "and you'll be a liability if we have to go in deeper."

"I'll go with Chavali." Eliot slid his sword back into its sheath. "You're better suited to brute force jobs. This one is more likely to be finesse."

Colby didn't like that idea either, but he sighed and nodded. "Alright, we'll go back the same way we came, and we'll wait on top of the wall, or on the other side if we need to."

While Colby and Railan made their way out, Eliot, Chavali, and Biholtz put as many pieces of the door inside the small cell as they could, to make it less obvious something happened to casual observation. With that done, they hurried back to the stairs and stood to one side while someone made their way up from the level below. They kept going farther up, not pausing at this floor. When that person was gone, Eliot looked back at Chavali.

"Do you have any ideas for figuring out where they are? I don't think taking the time to go through the whole place is a good idea."

Chavali turned to Biholtz, clasped her hand tightly. "Listen to me, Biholtz. Did Haizea or Danel ever say anything about where they were, what their room was like, what they saw, anything like that?" She let the thoughts wash over her as Biholtz rifled through her memories. What they were doing to her was avoided as if it was nothing more than rocks to be hopped over. The parts where she saw Haizea or Danel were shining moments she recalled easily.

The meetings happened every three days if she behaved, some of the times were longer than that because the girl resisted. She remembered the children as happy, both to see her and as if they were being treated well. They spoke about wondrous toys and nice ladies who helped them do things, and the food was yummy. Haizea was learning Shappan quickly now. It wasn't clear if they were being taken outside to play or not, but seemed in good health.

A voice startled them both, it was someone on the stairs calling out for help. That person going up must have come across the man Colby knocked out. They didn't pick him up and move him when they passed him again, so he must have still been lying there. It was a miracle the man wasn't noticed sooner, really. Eliot made a face, he probably hoped Colby would move the man on his way up with Railan.

"We should try down," Chavali hissed. "It is only a guess, though."

He nodded his agreement. "Up isn't an option right now anyway." With him in the lead, they ran down the stairs. His chain armor jangled, but it was quiet, muffled by the clothes he wore over it. Neither Chavali nor Biholtz had anything to make noise on them, it was just cloth swishing and footsteps from them. The next floor lower was the end of the stairs. Eliot peered around the edge of the wall, then they hurried along down a single hallway.

It was another dank stone corridor, and if Haizea and Danel were down here, Chavali didn't feel she'd caused enough harm to this place yet for the crime of keeping children like this, and for whatever they were doing to Biholtz. These people were animals, monsters, if they thought this was acceptable. She didn't care if the room was covered in soft things and they had all the toys and food they could possibly want—it was demented to keep children away from fresh air and sunshine, to force them to stay in one small place and never be free.

Unlike the upper floor, it was dark here. Eliot pulled out a glowing rock and held it high to light the way for them. No doors lined the walls at all. That was odd, but they found one at the other end. He held out a hand for them to stay back. Chavali put an arm around Biholtz and held her several steps away from the man as he knelt at the door and started using tools to inspect and tinker with it.

"Outsiders are strange," Chavali muttered. Who puts a long hallway at the bottom of a set of stairs like this? The only thing she could imagine was some sort of rock formation that made it necessary, but even that seemed silly. Once they found it, why not abandon this level and put things higher up? She shook her head and put it out of her mind as a peculiarity of telepaths. "What were they doing to you?"

Biholtz hugged Chavali back, calmer now than she was upstairs. "They said they were trying to draw out my potential. That it would work if only I stopped resisting. I don't know what that means, though. I wasn't resisting anything."

"That man was after me." He reached into her mind, so she assumed he understood how it worked, at least as well as she did. But, maybe he didn't. "Potential," she echoed. Of course. Eliot was right. He figured it might be hereditary, that another member of the clan, a younger, more pliant member, could be forced to develop the same or a similar ability. If it didn't work with Biholtz, he had two backups to try. "He doesn't realize it's through spirits," she murmured.

"I think he thinks you're my mother, maybe even for all three of us."

Chavali snorted a little. "Stupid Outsider."

Eliot was done, he waved them forward and opened the door. Grasping the handle with one hand, he stuffed his glowing rock into his bag with the other. He took a deep breath and pushed the door open. Beyond it was a large room with nothing but rows of beds. Several of the beds had occupants, of many different ages. There were both males and females, humans, elves, and half-breeds, even other races Chavali didn't have names for. Most of them were young, in their teens or less, but a few were adults.

Along with the twenty or so people lying on the beds, two women were also in the room, one of them spoon feeding an elf child, the other carrying a tray. Both looked up and were definitely surprised to see Eliot. Neither he nor Chavali paused at the threshold, they kept walking right in.

"Who are you?" The woman with the tray was closer, she stopped and faced them squarely, sternly. "What are you doing down here?"

Eliot pulled one of his swords out, not saying a word, stalking towards the woman.

"Wait," Chavali said, letting go of Biholtz so she could put a hand on Eliot's arm. "We need information." She regarded the woman with the tray, whose eyes were wide and frightened now. She was about ready to drop her tray, scream, and run like a flushed rabbit at the slightest provocation. "My children are down here. I do not care what you are doing to the rest of these people, I only want the ones that are mine. Tell me what you are doing to them."

The other woman stood and put her hands up in surrender. "We only tend them, that's all. We're not in charge here. Without us, they'll starve to death."

Tray Woman nodded slowly. "We're not doing anything to them."

The other woman pointed at two small figures on beds far away from the doors. "Those two must be yours."

Chavali grabbed Biholtz's hand again and pulled her that way. Yes, those two were Haizea and Danel, lying there, eyes closed, motionless but for breathing. "Why are they like this? What is happening to them?" As she got closer, she could see their eyes moving like they were dreaming.

The other woman gulped nervously. "They're in stasis. Their minds are active but their bodies are still. We didn't do it to them, and don't have a way to get them out. We're just servants, please don't hurt us."

Tearing her eyes away from the two small bodies, children she'd held in her lap, told stories to, watched since they were born, she stared hard at the other woman, not sure if she believed that or not. Simple servants, in the belly of a compound run by telepaths for whatever insanity this was, doing nothing more than caring for their victims. It sounded preposterous.

In her periphery, Chavali saw Eliot move, then the tray clattered to the floor, attracting her attention. When she looked, Tray Woman slumped to the floor, Eliot watched her impassively, his blade slick with blood again. "That is *not* an excuse for this. You had a choice. You made the wrong one."

The other woman's expression went flat and she threw her hands out. It wasn't shocking she assessed Eliot as the threat here. He bent as if suddenly subjected to a strong wind. Tiny cuts appeared on his exposed flesh and rents in his clothing, an assault by hundreds of invisible sharp things. For this woman, one harming clan who managed to trick her for at least a short time, Chavali had no problem deciding what to do. She was only a half step behind Biholtz as both of them ran to the woman.

Biholtz threw a punch to the woman's gut, Chavali threw an arm around her neck from behind and pulled. Either action separately might have been brushed aside by the woman, but both together was enough to break her concentration. Eliot growled angrily as he surged up and rushed forward, sword first. He plunged it into her belly and ripped it out the side, a furious rage on his face. It faded quickly as he panted, watching the woman fall to the floor.

Chavali watched her, too, but only long enough to be sure she wasn't going to get back to her feet and do something else. That only took a few seconds, then she hurried back to the space between the two beds with Haizea and Danel on them. "How do we free them?"

Biholtz gulped and shut her eyes, took a few steps back from the body. "I don't know."

"You escaped that other dream world thing, maybe you can pull them out of this one." Eliot reversed his grip on his sword and plunged it into the woman's heart. "I'd like to free all these people, but I have no idea how we'd get them out. By the time we can get back to the Tower and get more Fallen organized to come retrieve them, I know they'll be gone." Yanking the blade back out, he stalked back to the first woman and did the same thing.

Chavali nodded. She agreed, with everything he said. This kind of an intrusion wouldn't go undetected for long. Already, they knew someone was here and causing some kind of trouble. "Getting ourselves out is already a challenge."

Eliot grabbed a sheet off an empty bed and used it to clean off his blade. "We're going to need a distraction. I have some experience with that. Biholtz, right?" The girl nodded. "You seem like maybe you know how to fight?"

Nodding again, Biholtz pointed at his sword. "I know how to use a smaller blade than that, and a spear."

His face twisting into a grim smile made fearsome by the tiny cuts still oozing blood, Eliot pulled out his second blade, the shorter one, and handed it to her. "Defend Chavali. I'm going back to see what I can set up to cover our exit. Chavali, do whatever you can to wake them up, but when I get back, if they aren't awake, we're just going to carry them."

Biholtz gave him a face set with determination. "She is my Seer, her life is worth more than mine."

"It is not," Chavali chided. "We are worth the same, now. Defend us both equally."

Eliot offered his hand to Biholtz, who looked at it uncertainly. She went to take it to shake, but he grasped her forearm, leading her to do the same. "We're all getting out of here. No unnecessary heroics."

Chavali didn't watch as he left Biholtz behind and suggested leaving the door open so she could see anyone coming. Her attention turned to the two children and what to do to wake them up. The most obvious thing was to touch them, but she couldn't reach both at once. She grabbed one bed and dragged it closer to the other, climbed onto them and sat herself between both, and placed her bare hands on both their bare arms at once. There wasn't time to handle them individually.

She was flooded with images and thoughts, similar ones from each child. As suspected, both were in some kind of dream, both overflowing with good things, and no bad things. Each had a version of their own mother, a child's version, each had toys, lush grass, delightful foods, bright sunshine, laughter. Each also had the four goats, which struck Chavali as both interesting and heart-wrenching. They kept her in their thoughts even though she wasn't really there.

But, she wasn't pulled into the dreams, she was merely a passive observer. Her mind couldn't reach in and do or say anything, she could only watch. They ran and played, they hugged their mothers, they picked flowers and grass and had no idea it wasn't real and should be resisted. The bond of clan wasn't enough to get through this, she needed something else, some sort of way for them to hear her. Which might be as simple a matter as speaking to them, something she'd done so many times for both, they might just accept her voice even though it came from the outside.

"Haizea, Danel, it's Chavali." The urge to speak softly was strong, but she pushed that aside. They needed to hear her, and there was a lot to cut through. "I know you can hear me, hear my voice. The place you're in, it's not real. You want to believe it's real, because it's happy and filled with good things. But it's not. What's real is painful, it hurts, and I wish it didn't." This wasn't working, she wasn't getting anything from either of them to suggest they could hear her.

She raised her voice, leaned closer. "Haizea, I am here. Danel, I am here. I came for you, for clan, because there is nothing that matters more to me than clan. I know it took me a long time, but it was a difficult road I had to walk to get here. The four goats were my guide, but they had to stop to help me, because I was hurt. The clan was hurt. You were hurt, too." The goats, Danel latched onto that thread. "Iparre, Hegoa, Ekia, and Mendeba—they're here for us, for clan. I'm here for you.

"Remember how you tugged on my feather, how it felt so different from what you expected? It was stiff and coarse, not soft. It sprang back into a curl even though you crunched it in your hand. You asked me what color it was, Danel, and I said I didn't know, I needed you to tell me. It's Chavali, Danel, your Seer. Estevior's soul is bound to mine and to yours through me. We are clan, Danel, you, me, and Biholtz and Haizea."

In the boy's dream, his mother changed. A pink feather slowly sprouted from her forehead like a flower growing very fast. It was always queer to see how someone else saw her; he identified her strongly by the feather, which seemed to be larger and more floral than it really was. The tattoo around it stood out much more starkly than it really did. Her features were otherwise similar enough to his mother's that nothing else about her face changed, but he gave her a necklace, one she didn't have anymore.

"Hear me, Danel, Haizea. I'm here, and I won't let you get hurt again." Part of her screamed in frustration that she would make such an idiotic pledge. The rest knew it was necessary right now. "I need you to wake up, though. Open your eyes, see the world around you for what it is: an illusion meant to keep you still. Like when Mendeba thought he could roll around forever in the sweet smelling clover. But he got hungry, didn't he? And then he ate the clover and it was gone. He was so sad. Hegoa had to tell him to get off his lazy bottom to find more. Get off your lazy bottoms and find what's good in life by doing, not by letting someone trick you into lying there like lumps."

To her immense relief, Danel opened his eyes and the fantasy land faded away from his thoughts. She let go of Haizea to take him up in her arms and hold him tightly while he broke into tears. "I'm sorry," he said, over and over, and she let him for a short time.

"It's okay, Danel," she told him softly, tucking her own tears back, "but I need your help. We have to wake Haizea. She's still stuck. Can you help me?"

The boy nodded and looked at the smaller girl. He sucked in a deep breath and shouted at her. "Haizea! Wake up! We have crackers!"

Chavali laughed and reached out to brush Haizea's hair gently.

"Haizea, it's Chavali, and I have a story for you, but you have to be out here to get it, not in there."

"We need to move, Chavali," Eliot's voice said urgently from the doorway. "Now. We can't do anything for these other people if we want to get out of here ourselves, so don't bother asking."

"Go," Chavali set Danel down, "Biholtz will help you. I need to carry Haizea." To her relief, the boy seemed to catch on to the gravity of the situation and ran to Biholtz, grabbing a fistful of her ragged skirt instead of demanding to hold her hand. Chavali picked the smaller girl up. It was no different than carrying a sleeping child, and she'd done that more than a few times. "I have your doll, Haizea," she told the girl, hoping she'd wake up still. "It's in my new home, waiting for you. We'll get there tonight, if we're lucky, or tomorrow. But you'll have to wake up to have it." The girl didn't stir.

Eliot led the way back down the hallway, Biholtz right behind him still with the sword in hand. Danel trailed her and Chavali followed, ready to help Danel if he stumbled. That was the best she could do here: tend the children. Somehow, someday, she would change that. Whatever it took, she would not let herself just be baggage again. In the clan, she was a princess, of sorts, but that was over. Now, she wasn't just the Seer, she was the only Elder. It was her duty to protect her clan, and she would do it. Somehow, someday, whatever it took.

They reached the stairs, Eliot met someone and stabbed them without allowing any sort of conversation. Biholtz rushed up to help, and her sword came away stained with blood, too. Chavali shifted Haizea to her hip and took Danel by the hand. He didn't need to be shielded from this, only kept from getting hurt—clan needed to see death sooner or later, needed to know what it was, needed to understand what was lost and how it happened. Later, they would speak of it, he would be made to understand. For now, they watched from behind while Eliot and Biholtz skewered a man in plain robes before he could truly react.

Up the stairs they went, as fast as they could. When they reached the ground floor, Chavali was panting. The place was lit up with a golden glow, the roar and crackle of fire nearby. Eliot must have started it. If it didn't kill them before they could manage to escape, it was a good distraction. She tightened her grip on Danel's hand, trying to ignore how terrified he was, and set off through the maze, keeping Biholtz in sight, trusting to Eliot to know which way to go. Vaguely, she heard shouting, it sounded far away and strange.

"We're going to be okay," she told Danel firmly as she ducked to avoid flames licking the ceiling. A door opened ahead, Eliot ducked out through it, Biholtz followed. Something—she had no idea what—made Chavali hesitate for a moment. She held Danel back just in time to keep him from being crushed by a beam as it fell across the hallway, trapping them the inside. Danel shrieked in terror, she squeezed his hand firmly. "Don't panic. There's another way."

Haizea lifted her head and blinked sleepily. "Chavali?"

"Yes, Haizea, I'm glad you're awake." This was not the best time for the girl to wake up, but she couldn't complain about it having happened. "Hold onto me, we're trying to get out."

"Chavali!" Biholtz's voice was at least as panicked as Danel's mind. "Are you okay?"

"Yes, we're fine," she called out. "The smoke is thick. Is there a window near here?"

"Go to your left, if you're facing the door. There's a window. I'll break it for you!"

Taking two steps back was all Chavali needed to see that wouldn't work. "It's blocked! We're going the other way." Without waiting for more from Biholtz, she pulled Danel in that direction, leaning down to get under the thick layer of smoke forming at the ceiling. They dodged another fallen beam, ran quickly past flames threatening to grab them. Finally, there was daylight, and she pulled Danel to it, out through the gaping hole in the wall.

It was the front door. This place didn't have a huge number of people, but what they did have was already working on filling buckets with water. There was Yvette sitting off to one side, coughing and unable to help. The rest of these people were able to do the work of putting out a fire. When the three of them emerged, a woman grabbed her immediately and helped her get out of the way only to look at her in confusion.

"Who are you?" Her grip tightened on Chavali's arm, the one holding Haizea.

"Clan," Haizea spat at the woman.

"Our Seer," Danel said with a scowl and stomped on the woman's foot.

Chavali might have added something else, but this was as good an opportunity as she was likely to get. There were at least a dozen people here, most—if not all—of them telepaths. Were they to put their minds to stopping her, they would. No reason to give them the opportunity to collect themselves that much. She pulled Danel along and ran for the next nearest one, bowling him over.

That wasn't going to be enough to get away, but it didn't need to be. Colby growled out a challenge, attracting attention to himself as he ran into the chaos, sword held high. Furious thumping on the front gate was followed by it flying open, Karias standing there after having just kicked it open with his rear legs. Biholtz ran in with Eliot, and Railan slipped around the edge of the mayhem to reach the front gate.

Chavali and Danel ran for the horse together, Haizea clinging to Chavali's shoulder. She didn't stop there, as much as Danel wanted to. The others would probably need the horse to help them get out, so she kept pulling the boy along, running as fast as he could manage down the path. The noise receded, the smell of smoke receded, the panic receded.

Chapter 15

Danel couldn't run for long, and neither could Chavali, especially not with a child in her arms. Slowing to a walk, she set the girl down and focused on catching her breath. "We can't stop, so we keep going, just slower."

"What about Biholtz?"

"She'll be fine. Eliot is my friend, he'll take care of her."

"You're bleeding." Danel pointed to her face.

Chavali reached up and brushed her face. Her fingers came away with smears of fresh blood from her cheek. "So I am. It's not serious, I'll be fine." Now that she knew about it, the small wound started to sting. Other aches and pains also chose to make themselves known. She groaned and rubbed her face, noticed there was a sore spot on her jaw. That flight through the fiery first floor was more painful than she thought.

Thundering hoof beats made them all turn. It was Karias, carrying Colby, going at full speed. The pair of them, like that, was a magnificent sight: a knight on his steed, charging to meet some challenge. The horse slowed as it got close, stopped a short distance behind them and turned, putting the two of them into a pose that made the sunlight glint off

Colby's armor.

Chavali wasn't sure if it was the horse or the rider who had a flair for the dramatic. "We're fine," she said before he could get anything out. "Is everyone out?" Haizea and Danel hid behind her, holding onto her skirts to peek around her.

He smiled at her and nodded. "Not just going to ask about Biholtz?"

"That would be suggesting she is the only one whose welfare is relevant."

Colby snorted in amusement, and the horse tossed his head. "Minor injuries only. We didn't kill everyone, either. They decided putting out the fire was more important than stopping us. The rest are behind me, on the road, I just wanted to make sure you weren't being carried off by rabid bears."

"That would be terribly rude of us, after all the trouble everyone just went to so we could escape." She laughed. It felt good.

"I agree," he said as he stepped down off the horse, making it look no more difficult than walking down stairs.

"Haizea, Danel, this is Colby. He is my friend and helped me find you." She reached back and brushed both small heads, tousling their hair.

"We met before, actually," Colby said as he stopped a few feet away and crouched down. "Only, we weren't properly introduced. I have some water you can drink, and if you want to ride the horse, I can help you up there."

"It is okay," Chavali said, trying to urge them to take the offer. "Karias is big and can beat down doors, but he is also gentle and can carry people. He was nice enough to let me ride him before, and you will not fall so long as you do not fall asleep." In the distance, she could see the other three getting closer. "Come, when Biholtz gets here, she will ride with you." The two children still hesitated, so she shooed Colby off a little and pulled both into a warm embrace.

"You are clan. I won't let you be carried away from me again. I don't know how you'll fit into the things I have to do now, but no matter what, I'll be there. I'll see you as often as I can, I'll tell you stories, and I'll wipe away your tears. Colby is a good man, and I trust him." She grinned. "His horse is a little weird, but that's not such a bad thing." Relieved they both found that funny, she nodded towards the beast. "We have a long way to go, it's too far for you both to walk the whole way yourselves."

Haizea kissed her cheek, Danel nodded stoically, then both children allowed Colby to lift them up onto Karias's broad back. As soon as Biholtz caught up, Chavali hugged her tightly, and she, too, was helped up.

"So long as there is clan, there is hope," Chavali said as she reached up and patted Haizea's foot. Biholtz covered the three of them with Chavali's cloak and the group set off at the best pace they could all manage. Railan was still exhausted and so was glad to keep it as slow as Chavali needed it to be. They plodded along for hours. The children insisted upon getting down to walk a few times, it was enough to perk everyone's spirits.

Though she was weary from the day and the cold, when Chavali— by then watching the ground go by her feet—heard Biholtz say, "I can see the light of a Creator's Tower," the pale blue glow in the distance made her want to press on. The sun was already setting, and they were still a good distance away, but it was a welcoming beacon announcing they weren't so far from home.

"I'm not sure I can make it that far without a rest," Railan said, sounding well and truly drained to her dregs.

Eliot grunted. "I'd rather go all night to be healed before I sleep than stop now."

"I would also prefer to keep going," Chavali nodded. She wasn't sure she'd make it that far either, especially with a blanket for a cloak, but not trying meant never finding out.

"You can ride with the children," Biholtz offered to Railan. "I can walk."

Colby helped them switch. Chavali pushed herself to walk with Biholtz, pitching her voice low so Haizea and Danel wouldn't overhear enough to understand while she spoke in the clan tongue. "Did you kill anyone?"

Biholtz frowned and nodded. "I didn't really have time to pay a lot of attention to it. Eliot kept going. It was hard to not stop and take notice. You killed someone too. Stabbed him through the neck."

"He was hurting you, I would have done worse things to him if I had time for it. For clan, there isn't anything that's too much or too cruel. What is done to one is done to all and returned in kind, with interest." This conversation should probably wait until she had a chance to rest. By then, though, Biholtz might come up with her own answers.

Chavali forced herself to nod with confidence and show the girl as much bravado as she could muster. "When I find that man who attacked our clan, he will feel the wrath of the Blaukenevs, keenly." In reality, he and what he'd done terrified her. The memories peeked out from where she'd stuffed them. She slammed the lid on that box shut again. Later, she might find a way to deal with them.

"It doesn't bother you that you killed someone?"

Chavali pursed her lips and tried to decide how to answer that. Biholtz wanted to be reassured she wasn't a bad person and that her Seer also wasn't a bad person. She also wanted to hear the truth. "Given the opportunity to do things differently, I wouldn't change that detail. So many things happened in there, though, and I'm tired, and I'm so happy to have the three of you back, that I haven't thought much about it yet." She took a heavy breath and gave the matter a small amount of consideration. "It's possible I could have just knocked him unconscious, but I don't really have the skill to do that in one stroke, and those who do were busy."

"I just stuck that guy with the sword." Biholtz looked at her hands in Chavali's mittens, turning them over a few times to see both sides. "There was no thinking. Or, I guess, I thought it was him or us. I wasn't mad at him, he was just in the way."

"The Elders questioned themselves, all the time, about everything they did. My father had doubts down to the core of his soul." This wasn't quite the same as what Biholtz asked, but it came close enough, and she was old enough to understand it. "I remember once winding up in his dreams by accident, and I saw how much he worried that the men he killed to protect the clan were stains on his soul, that Estevior would frown down on him for being too cruel or too kind, all of that. That shook me to the core, learning he wasn't perfect all the time. But at least I knew I didn't have to be, either."

Biholtz went quiet, thinking. Chavali was too tired to continue in this vein anyway, so it was for the best. After a few minutes, though, she asked about something else. "What happened to you? He said you were dead. I felt—I don't know."

"You felt the death of your Seer." Ten years ago, Chavali felt that when Marika passed. It didn't last long, because Chavali became the Seer as soon as the feather was ready, but it was like having an arm chopped off for that time between. "It's complicated, and I'm not up to the explanation right now. What matters is that I'm here now."

"A clan of four." Biholtz pronounced it like a death sentence.

"When I woke up, I thought it was a clan of one." Chavali smiled, still somewhat stunned by the good fortune of finding them so quickly, and having such success against terrible odds. "Four is a lot more than one. Danel and Haizea, when they're older, will have a brood. If you want to bring someone in and have babies in a few years, you can help with it. There will be a clan again, it'll just take time."

That made Biholtz go quiet again, and they plodded onwards well into the night, walking straight towards the soft blue light that seemed to always be another mile or two away. Finally, though, they were close, then they were inside and Eliot spoke with the guardians. Colby activated the Tower to send them closer to home. The storm had passed, and the paths around the Tower were clear.

Haizea and Danel were too tired to keep going. Chavali plodded, ready to fall over. Railan was no better off. Eliot and Biholtz both stumbled. Colby's weariness seemed much less than everyone else's, though he kept yawning and rubbing his face on the sleeve under his arm guard. "I can ride ahead, see about getting some horses or a wagon here for all of you, or we can just camp here for the night." He pointed to one of the rough shelters nearby, just like at the other Tower.

"Ride ahead," Chavali answered immediately. "I am concerned for Haizea to sleep in the cold like this. We don't have enough supplies." No one else said anything, and as Colby mounted up and urged his horse to speed him home, she picked up Danel and put his weight mostly on her hip, and pointed for Biholtz to carry the smaller girl. "We walk until he meets us. Home is not far."

Eliot grunted and pushed himself up under Railan's arm to support her. "I don't want to, but she's right. We should keep moving. Once I stop, I'm not going to want to start again."

"When we get there," Railan sighed, "we're going to have to go down all those stupid stairs."

Chavali snorted. "At least it is not up all those stupid stairs."

"That's something, I suppose." Railan chuckled.

Eliot grunted again. "I don't mind the stairs so much, it's those first two levels where it just feels like they're there for no reason other than to get in the way. Which, of course, they are."

Railan giggled without sounding girlish or high-pitched. "I have no idea why that's funny," she choked out between chortles, "but it is."

"Because you're overtired, ya dope." Shrugging his shoulder to shove her, Eliot shook his head. "Blew yourself out blowing that guy's face out."

This was too much for Railan, who now laughed so much she couldn't walk properly. Chavali found no humor in the situation and kept slogging onward with Biholtz, the children draped over them like sacks of potatoes. It was too much effort to talk now, so neither of them did. Just when Chavali was thinking she might drop Danel, she heard hoof beats. There was Colby on his horse again already, leading another horse, a woman behind him on another horse leading two more.

Words were unnecessary. The woman stopped for them, Colby kept going. Chavali and Biholtz climbed up on the more normal sized mounts and rode the rest of the way. It took only a short time, then she was carrying Danel downstairs, remembering to count the floors. Hers took too long to reach, but then she was counting doors. Her door was ajar, just as she left it. The four of them piled onto the bed without doing more than pulling shoes off.

When Chavali woke to the sound of knocking on her door and stirring at her back. Pulling herself free of the tangle made of her whole clan would take some effort. Not yet awake enough to attempt it, she stayed in the pile. "Come in," she called out.

Haizea's little voice grumbled sleepily, Biholtz yawned and stretched, Danel made a soft little snorting noise. Eliot opened the door and carried a tray in. "I hope you got enough rest. Since this was your first mission, and we were all a wreck when we got back, I brought you all some breakfast. It's probably not close to being enough, but it's a start."

Chavali rubbed her eyes and sat up, looking him over. The tray looked to be piled high with bread and fruit and juice. "This is a nice thing, thank you."

He nodded in acknowledgment, his eyes taking in the sight of the four of them, all stirring and in different stages of waking. "As soon as you're up to it, Eldrack wants to see you." She noticed his gaze lingered on herself more than the others. That didn't bother her, though she couldn't remember him seeming interested much before.

Gesturing to her face, she asked, "You are healed?"

"Yeah," he smiled, probably pleased she thought to ask. "I saw a Healer before I found my bed last night. If you need one, just go down to the fourteenth level. They mostly stay lower, but you can always find one or two lurking there to tend minor injures."

"This is good to know, thank you."

"Oh," he set the tray down on her table and pulled a few things out of his pockets. "I picked these things up in the room where Biholtz was being kept. I didn't know if they belong to any of you, but figured you have nothing, so something is more than you've got." He set a pouch and something shiny beside the tray.

Haizea sat up and stretched her little arms, her mouth yawned wide. Biholtz slid off the bed. Eliot seemed to take all of this as a reason to leave and smiled at her more broadly, then gave them all a polite, friendly bow, and left the room.

"He likes you," Biholtz said with a grin as she reached the tray and grabbed food to stuff it in her mouth.

Chavali rolled her eyes. "I'm not interested." She gently shoved Danel and Haizea with one hand for each. "Get up, eat." Following them, she ignored the food in favor of the pouch and what turned out to be a gold disc when she got closer. It was her necklace, the chain gone but the pendant intact. The pouch was not hers, but she upended it on the table to reveal it contained all of her bones and stones and crystals. Several needed tending, the ink all but washed away and edges chipped or worn.

"They tried to use them on me," Biholtz said after swallowing a bite of bread.

Chavali ran her fingers over several and frowned. "Use them? How?"

The girl shrugged. "Me touching them, them touching them while also touching me, chanting, all kinds of things."

"Idiots." Picking one up, she rubbed her fingers on it. The contours and rune markings were familiar and grounding.

"You should eat, too, Chavali," Biholtz said with a note of chiding in her voice.

"This tastes funny," Haizea said, wrinkling up her nose.

"Outsiders don't know how to cook properly." Chavali chuckled, picking up the doll from her dresser. The girl hadn't noticed it yet. "I wish I also had something for you both," she told Danel and Biholtz, "but this was all they saved."

Haizea squealed in delight and jumped up to take the doll, hugging her leg. "Bapi!"

"It's okay." Biholtz nudged Danel, who nodded sullenly. "I'll show Danel how to make his own sword."

The boy looked up and smiled. "A real one?"

Chavali grinned and nodded. "It depends on what they have here, but at least a wood one. When you get good with that, we'll get you a metal sword, just like your papá's." Their faces fell, but the loss wasn't so keen and recent for them. All three had lost their clan months ago. She crouched down enough to be closer to Haizea's and Danel's level.

"They're in here," she said, pointing to her forehead, then to theirs.

"They're in here," she pointed to her chest, and also to theirs. "We remember them, so they live on. We will meet new people, we will love them like clan, and we will move on, but we will never forget. It's okay to miss them, to wish they were here with us in person. Just know they are here with us in memories." All three nodded their solemn understanding and dug back into the food.

Chavali only took enough to silence her stomach, not wanting to keep Eldrack waiting too long. After showing the children to the washroom, she left Biholtz supervising the two younger ones in baths to find him. Someone directed her to his office on the thirteenth floor. This direction didn't help, as she still couldn't see the numbers. By asking a few other people along the way, she wound up in the right place.

His office was sparsely furnished with a desk, three chairs, a potted plant in one corner, a bookshelf with various oddments, and a wooden file cabinet. A small bowl on his desk held the room's magical light source. The man himself seemed well rested. He looked up from writing something, then smiled at seeing her. "I understand the mission went well, if a little more destructively than intended." Setting his pen down, he gestured to the nearest chair, the one facing his desk.

"The clan is four," Chavali nodded. "They seem well. I will spend some time to determine what was done to them and try to fix it."

"Of course, they're your family. If they need help beyond what you can provide, please ask."

She knew he had some other reason for wanting to see her even without the subtle cues he threw. "I will do my best to remember this offer."

He nodded and clasped his hands together. Something in the set of his shoulders announced he had bad news. "Unfortunately, they can't stay with you down in the Tower."

"Why not?" Chavali scowled at him, ready to unleash a torrent of venom in his direction.

"Because this isn't a place for children." He put up a hand to stop her before she could form a full reaction. "We'll place them with a family on the surface, in the village that camouflages the entrance to this facility. You'll be able to spend time with them every day while you're here. I won't deny you access to them, I just can't have them running around down here. There are far too many ways they could get hurt, and far too many people who just don't want to deal with young children among the Fallen." Something about the second point piqued her curiosity. He meant this in more than one way. She would seek the reason later.

"I see." If she could see them every day, then it wasn't really so different from being with the clan. Except that she liked waking up like that this morning, in a pile of warm bodies. "What about Biholtz? She is twelve."

Eldrack pursed his lips and thought for a few seconds. "Does it not seem prudent to keep the three of them together on the surface? Chavali, I can appreciate what it must be like to have the last of your family with you, but you can't take care of them and train and go on missions, and do the other things you'll need to do. I'll make sure that whoever they stay with, they're capable, and won't mind you dropping in whenever you can. They can stay with you today and tonight, but they'll have to go to the surface tomorrow."

She wanted to curse him and call him all kinds of very unpleasant things, but he was right. Just a little bit, she hated him for being right. If she was going to keep her promise to herself, to never be a bystander again, she needed time not worrying about them. She could see them every day she was here. That would be enough. Nodding in acceptance, she noticed he relaxed quite a bit. "Was there anything else?"

"No, that's it for now." He smiled at her, sympathetic and friendly. "Unless you wanted to ask me any questions while you're here?"

Shaking her head, she stood up. Too many things had happened and she needed time to think. There would be questions, and many of them, but not now. She took two steps away, then stopped and turned back. "Thank you. For letting me go to get them."

"It was the only choice I could truly make."

Chavali nodded and left the office, thinking about how to tell Biholtz, Haizea, and Danel, how to mark the walls so she didn't have to count everything all the time, and how to keep her promise. A lot of work lay ahead of her, but she felt secure in the knowledge that she had clan and they were safe. So long as they had each other, they had everything they truly needed.

About the Authors

Lee French lives in Worcester, MA with two kids, two mice, two bicycles, and too much stuff. She is an avid gamer and active member of the Myth-Weavers online RPG community, where she is known for her fondness for Angry Ninja Squirrels of Doom. In addition to spending much time there, she also trains year-round for the one-week of glorious madness that is RAGBRAI, has a nice flower garden with absolutely no lawn gnomes, and tries in vain every year to grow vegetables that don't get devoured by neighborhood wildlife.

She is an active member of the Northwest Independent Writer's Association and one of two Municipal Liaisons for the Olympia region of NaNoWriMo.

Erik Kort abides in the glorious Pacific Northwest, otherwise known as Mirkwood-Without-The-Giant-Spiders, though the normal spiders often grow too numerous for his comfort. He is defended from all eight-legged threats by his brave and overly tolerant wife, and is mocked by his obligatory writer's cat. When not writing, Erik comforts the elderly, guides youths through vast wildernesses, and smuggles more books into his library of increasingly alarming size.

Thanks for reading! If you liked this book, please take a minute to post a review of it wherever you buy your books.

www.authorleefrench.com   www.tangledskypress.com

Made in the USA
Middletown, DE
30 June 2015